THE FIFTH STATION

David —

The great energy in your work is married to great compassion — A remarkable gift.

I wish you good fortune, my friend.

MC

Breadloaf ?
8-95

A NOVEL BY KEVIN McILVOY

THE FIFTH STATION

Kevin McIlvoy (signature)

ALGONQUIN BOOKS OF CHAPEL HILL 1988

Published by
Algonquin Books of Chapel Hill
Post Office Box 2225
Chapel Hill, North Carolina 27515-2225

in association with
Taylor Publishing Company
1550 West Mockingbird Lane
Dallas, Texas 75235

Parts of this novel first appeared, in different
form, in *Portland Review*, *Telescope*, and *MSS*.

The author thanks Dan Ursini, Ken Smith,
Rick Russo, Ann Rohovec, Ken Kuhlken, and
Robert Houston; The Family Inn, for the
table in the corner and the refills; New
Mexico State University, for the freedom to
risk the three-point shots. And Margee,
Colin, and Paddy for believing,
morning after morning.
This work was supported by a grant from the
National Endowment for the Arts.

Design by Molly Renda.

LIBRARY OF CONGRESS CATALOGING-IN-PUBLICATION DATA

McIlvoy, Kevin, 1953–
    The fifth station: a novel / Kevin McIlvoy.

    p.   cm.
    ISBN 0-912697-76-8
    I. Title.
PS3563.C369F5   1988
813'.54-dc 19   87-26452

FIRST EDITION

Friend, I said, lend me three loaves.
And I was given as many as I needed.

LUKE XI

THE FIFTH STATION

The Cyrenian Helps Jesus Carry His Cross

THE WAY OF THE CROSS

1

It won't make a difference to write down here that I was the reason my younger brother, Matthew, died. My father, who never knew it, is dead. My mother, who knows it, who has been broken by it, writes me, her youngest now at thirty-two years of age, from Illinois. She says all the misery of the world walks along the Way of the Cross to Calvary. And she prays my older brother Luke and I "will soon understand."

I toast Jesus. Bottoms up to the Son of God.

Luke's a street bum, a hobo here in Las Almas. I never need to be reminded that he knows how Matthew died. Cheers to my fellow drunks, Matthew and my father, impaled on bottles to my left and right. I forgive your sins. Surely you will be with me in hell this very day.

None of this can make a difference. But I have to get it down: how it could have been. I *have* to remember how it was the day he died. His words, maybe. Maybe, his open eyes.

At the steel mill the high-risk jobs pay twenty-six cents more an hour. That's about two extra dollars a shift, but then you usually get overtime on those jobs, so with the double-time it adds up. We were told the big, nine-story smokestacks at the hot strip mill would need to have their brick insides torn out, and we sat in the bar You Dam Right after the four-to-twelve shift discussing whether we wanted to volunteer for the job the next day. Our foreman said he thought it was work that was only done every thirty years or so. Old-timers at the mill said they never heard of it being done ever.

Matthew said, "We're talking about—let's see—probably an extra forty bucks." Three years out of high school, he had that high school enthusiasm, my brother. He had a sharp mind that nothing could ever dull. And he was probably the finest athlete Meltenville ever produced. "Between us," he said, "it'd be a hundred and fifty-some bucks total for the night if they double us over." We always figured our income that way—as the total between us. We had plans to open a sign-painting shop all our own somewhere away from the steel mill that ground my father and his father and grandfather into just enough dust to bury us too. In another year we'd have enough saved to leave Illinois for New Mexico, where Luke was.

The year didn't sound like so long a time to either of us that afternoon. We shot pool and talked about it with Stan Lipiniski and Howard Paskas, who were just off work from the blooming mill. We didn't bet on the pool game but we won so often Stan and Howard started running out of quarters to feed the table. I said I'd get some change, but Howard, whose work goggles had worn an extra line under his already line-worn eyes, said to save it. "We don't want you leaving letters off your signs out West just for lack of paint, huh, Stan?" Stan, a Pole, hardly ever understood English, which was made from sounds weaker, after all, than the sounds of the slab shearer he operated.

In his usual thick soup of clichés, Stan said, "No sir you bet not on your life one bit!"

Matthew's laughter was soft, I guess because he knew Stan and had worked with him before we were moved to the hot strip. Guys like Matthew and me, who could speak some Polish, usually worked with Stan so he didn't get instructions wrong and hurt himself.

"Sure don't want no signs," said Howard, "that say 'urger King,' do we?"

Stan's face was a question mark. He said, "Damn right by God." Stan understood Matthew's laughter. I mean, he understood he wasn't being laughed *at.* Matthew had seen him through his greenhat days and into the union, and would let his lunch sit if Stan came to him with a question.

"I've been thinking about that," Matthew said. "If we're going to mix our own paint to save money, we're going to have to study up."

I groaned. "They've got mixing charts and things, don't they?"

Howard racked the balls and rolled the cue ball down the table to me. "You painting the bell on the Taco Bell or shooting?"

"The moon," said Stan who could enjoy a laugh as good as the next guy.

When they left an hour later, we were still drinking, playing eight ball, and forgetting who was shooting stripes and who had solids.

Matthew told me I'd better learn to book up because I'd have to be a regular paint-scholar Ph.D. "That's for sure you're right about that and don't I know it!" I said. By that time pool was hopeless.

Laughter's a good way to know you've drunk too much. You get that feeling that your hand won't lift a glass of ice but your insides are like cork. You laugh and feel your heart and guts bob inside you and you know: too much. I bought a straight-up Johnny Walker Red and one for Matthew and looked at the big spring water Budweiser clock and said, "Two-thirty! In the morning!"

Matthew put his arm on my shoulder and I hitched my hand on his there. We're not a family that hugs. Not the McWelts. So, it always felt good to be drunk enough to put our arms around each other.

"A miracle," I said, looking at the bright plastic water flowing out of the clock on the wall of Knud Hildebrandt's bar. "You closed?" I asked Knud, who was wiping tables around us.

"Half an hour ago," Knud said. "Take him home, Matthew." It was what he always said. He'd known our dad and grandfather. I always wondered if he had let *them* stay past closing time too. But I never asked because it made me mad having somebody tell my little brother to take his big brother home. Couldn't he see Matthew was just as smashed as me?

"Sell us some cigarettes," said Matthew. Knud gave us a

pack. We probably all but kissed him, like drunks will do for the smallest favor.

I pointed at the perfect stream of water on the wall. "The miracle of Budweiser. Turning water into beer."

Knud pulled the plug.

"A miracle," said Matthew, looking away.

I helped Matthew out of his chair. "See you later, Knud. Or earlier. We're going to tear out the inside throat of that smokestack." I pointed out his neon-green window at the sky. "The nine-story one."

Matthew said, "You damn right!" We laughed at the stupid joke, the bar's favorite overused joke.

"Good night," said Knud, not laughing.

We were so wet-eyed with our funniness, we forgot to pay our tab. We walked the eight blocks to the 20th Street railroad crossing and another four blocks to our apartment on Sherman, then got our money. Bounce-passing a basketball between us, we walked back through the rotten ice-cold weather. A couple of times one of us missed a pass so we had to go into the street. Finally, we just charged down the middle of 20th, passing the ball, fumbling and staggering, but not falling even once. Knud had closed up the bar.

It's a slow acid, booze. But if your work so completely wastes you that—drunk or not—you can always eat and—drunk or not—you can sleep, how do you know the acid's burning you away at the nerves and eyes, and how do you know it's burning away your will to do anything but dream and drink and work some more in order to dream and drink?

At four a.m. after Matthew fell asleep, I called Homer, the hot roll finishing foreman on the graveyard shift, and asked him to save the smokestack work for Matthew and me on Christmas.

"Dangerous," he said. "You know that."

"Twenty-six extra cents an hour's worth."

He grunted. "McWelts," he said, like he was writing it down. Even over the phone I could hear the slabs boom onto the platforms in the ovens and scream as they were pressed through the rollers.

"Overtime?" I asked.

"Sure."

"Double time?"

He agreed to that. He was a nice man, Homer; so protective that some called him Homo. But only behind his back. When I thanked him, he said we could kiss his feet when we came in at noon. "Each toe, boys."

Growing up in Meltenville we knew lots of guys like Homer. My mom's friends were church friends or cousins or mothers she met through her children's playmates. My dad's friends came from everywhere: steelworkers, barmates, butchers, old class buddies, ex-bosses, and vets. He could easily get genuinely close to the salesman at the Spalding's Sport and Trophy, where my brothers and I bought our letter sweaters and where our winner's plaques and statues were engraved with our name or school name.

When Luke was still working at the blast furnace, we lived within ten blocks of the mill. A long time ago. St. Louis was a bridge away. The St. Louis Arch, the Gateway to the West, was finished around the time I was twelve and Matthew was nine, but it was more awesome incomplete than when it was complete. Big as a tennis court, a sign short of the McKinley bridge had Stan the Man Musial on it. His head was tilted back, his eyes following the place far beyond the sign where the home-run hit was headed. Above Jack Buck and Harry Carey floated the neon words, "It's A Home Run!!!" The exclamation points were baseball bats; the periods, baseballs. Not far from the Baseball Cardinals sign, but blocked by brick two-stories, was a Mobil station. From our house we couldn't see the station itself but couldn't miss the winged horse above it, turning slowly and powerfully, high in the air.

A block south of us lived our grandmother and grandfather. We had a neighbor, next door, who kept our basketballs when they strayed over her high Cyclone fence. Kept them right on her back porch just to show us. Another neighbor stole them back for us just to show *her*. And behind us, across a deep, narrow alley, we had a neighbor who liked to drink. My dad drank with him almost every weekend. Bottles set down between them on a carpenter's workbench, they drank and worked on "projects" and never finished the cabinets, the sewing tables, the chairs, or anything, but got slobbery drunk. They showed *everybody*.

At dinnertime, Mom would send me to get Dad. "Just him," she'd say, because he'd often bring Mr. Paschowski home to tumble his food off the table and talk football and blow his nose in his balled-up napkin.

"Just him, Michael," she'd say. "Please." She wouldn't let Matthew come with me.

I couldn't do any good. At the back door to our kitchen, Dad and Joe Paschowski would lean on the chains of the hanging porch rocker. We would stop to smell the oxtail soup and the strong tea before Dad banged his fist on the screen-door frame.

"Mike here," he'd say to Mother, "undered if Joe could have dinner ith us." When he was most drunk he always dropped *w*s; he would form the *w* with his lips, but then was incapable of the necessary push of air.

I would helplessly shake my head and shrug to show Mother I had tried to bring only Dad. Matthew would say, "Boy, oh boy" in that wiseass way that was already too full of irony for a nine-year-old.

Afterward, after the floor and table were puddled with his soup and tea, Mr. Paschowski would clear his sinuses, ball his napkin up and, gripping it tightly in his palm, solemnly say, "Patricia, I thank you."

"Underful soup," Dad would say. "You think so, Mike?" If I didn't give him an answer, he could get one from Matthew. "Right, Dad."

Then the two men would talk about Unitas's arm or argue about how the season was going to size up or, if a game or a fight was on television, they would go to Joe's to watch it.

Booze helps me forget distinctions between the truth and the exaggerated truth, so less is required for me to remember.

Basketballs. They always help. A workbench I have brought all the way to New Mexico with me.

Another thing: a quilt my mother took twelve years to make. Barely contained in each large white panel of it is a whorl of blossoming American Red Rose. When I pull

my knees up and cradle my head on the quilt, I can make
a warm mound of earth to sink into.

This was a long time ago.

Luke had accepted a basketball scholarship at SIU-
Edwardsville and was commuting to campus from his apart-
ment out behind the Siebold Grocery on Madison Avenue.
He didn't visit too often.

That Thanksgiving he had planned on coming over,
but canceled at the last minute. When I had to go tell Dad
dinner was ready, he and Joe sent me away. "Mike," Joe
said, "inform your dear mother we'll be arriving shortly
before the fourth quarter." He talked that deliberate way, I
was told, because he had been a judge once. I didn't believe
it then. I don't know what I believe now.

When I returned home and told her what Joe had said,
she turned away from me. "It's already two-thirty," she said.
"I wish just once." She spoke into the screen door facing the
alley. "Just once."

As far as I could tell, it was the one thing she said more
often than anything else. To try understanding him, I stud-
ied her. In our neighborhood of broad-shouldered, noble
Polish women, she was an exception: her character conveyed in a slighter frame, in thinner arms and smaller
hands; her shoulders narrow and bowed a little, her face
missing the impressive marble resolve of the Polish women.
It could be a stern face when she corrected those who
assumed incorrectly she was Polish. "I am," she politely told
them, "Lithuanian."

Matthew and I came in from practicing hook shots and

we drank some milk. Matthew said he didn't like blue milk. She said he was welcome to have water if two percent wasn't good enough for him. "God," he said. She looked bullets at him and said, "You can eat soap if you don't watch out."

The turkey was odd-smelling. When I said as much, she frowned at me.

At three o'clock, waiting for them to come, we set out the butter and bread and poured the iced tea. "What do you think?" she asked. She was referring to the table, but I had half answered her before I realized that. "They'll be here right away," I said. "Mr. Paschowski said before the. . . ."

For the next half hour we talked about the Thanksgiving mass, and Matthew complained about how long high masses were; she said they were ceremonies and ceremonies were meant to be long. Wasn't Father Luzinski looking bad these days, she asked, and wanted to know who would replace him, as if Matthew and I could possibly know. Like some kind of predictable feint before the outside jump shot, this patter was usually a sign.

She reminded us that Grandmother was also ill and that it must have been the first time in a long time Grandmother had missed a high mass. Our Aunt Norma had brought Thanksgiving dinner to her and Grandfather. We'd visit them after our meal, "if it's not too late," she said, her fisted hands disappearing into her apron pockets. We heard Dad's voice and his laughter.

"Pat, put the dinner down," he said from the alley. "Our chops have been set and aiting on the first score." He placed his arm around Joe's shoulder and heralded him in through the screen door. He held a chair out for him. "Judge Joseph Paschowski presiding!" he said. Though he was gifted with the Irish instinct for making kings of his friends, he treated none so grandly as Mr. Paschowski. When Dad moved to kiss her on the mouth, Mom offered a cold cheek to him.

He sat down. "They're knee-deep in mud and moving no air a yard at a time, boys, and I never—" But as she placed the main course on the table, he stopped. He ran his hands over the hair at his temples and his smile suddenly stood in awkward contrast to the straight lines forming around it. Bumping the table away from him, he said, "Patricia?" He stared at the serving dish. "It's ham."

"Yes," Mother said. By seating herself, she both challenged him and backed away from him.

"You know damn ell Joe can't eat that!" He pointed at it as if at a horror.

Scored into diamonds, topped with two big pineapple slices, two bright red maraschino eyes, and a glaze of brown sugar, it looked and smelled exactly like what it was: the forbidden food. The food we all, Dad included, loved and never ate because our visitor for every Christian holiday meal was Jewish. Kosher, so he said.

Joe mumbled something about knowing when he was not welcome and wishing he had known before. His face contracted with genuine disappointment.

"You think this is funny?" Dad asked her. "You think I have to put up with this crap?" When she didn't answer, he said, "I don't! By God, I don't!" I had never seen him so wild with rage though I had seen him rip an unironed shirt in two and try to kick the President out of the radio.

Once, at three in the morning, I had seen him lean over Mrs. Roczyky's fence and scream at the top of his lungs, "Give us our goddamn basketballs back!" Though many times I had heard him ask, "You think I have to put up with this crap?" it had never run me through with such fear.

"Matthew," he said, "you know about this?" He leaned over the table, and his expression changed. Matthew was his closest ally among his three sons. Sadly now, he said, "You did. You did, huh?" Matthew was unable to shake his head no. I remembered how, earlier, I had smelled ham.

Mr. Paschowski gripped the edge of the table and then stood. "I got—I'd better—"

Mother finally spoke. "Yes, Joe. Let's let this one meal be ours."

"What?" Dad asked. "What!"

"Just this once," she said. "Please." The word was his invitation to explode. That was always true. It always amazed me how, knowing that, she would say the word. Surely she must have known it.

Dad was circling the table to reach her when Mr. Paschowski said, "My dear boys." I held open the screen door for him. We followed him and then stood in our backyard averting our eyes from him where he had stopped in the alley. Our neighbor Mr. Mihalich, the man who stole back our basketballs, was on his back porch. "You all right?" he asked.

The voice calmed Joe. He pulled his shirtsleeves over his wrists. "Of course," he said, and walked slowly to his house.

"You boys," Mihalich asked, "you okay?"

Impossible to answer that. When Mr. Paschowski was gone, we went into the garage and sat on the hood of the car. I heard the screen door slam and Dad cross the alley to Joe's. I imagined he would tell Mr. Paschowski that it was an accident, that she forgot. Just forgot. Then, Dad's laughter would set things right.

"There he goes," said Matthew.

"Kyrie eleison," I said.

"Christe eleison," he said. (We were both server boys at the mass.) The sacrilege made us feel better.

On the wall shelves around us hung car guts of every kind: an assortment of rubber hoses and mufflers, a dozen or more batteries, belts, gaskets, disassembled engine parts. A Snap-On tool chest stood in one corner.

Moonlighting from the steel mill, Dad had been a mechanic, though not for long. At first, our backyard had been lined up with cars needing repair because word spread in town that he was cheap and quick. Then, so I've been told, the fruits of his labor began to show up broken down on driveways and road shoulders and condemned to junkyards. When word spread *why* he was so quick and why so cheap, we could play again in the backyard "whenever you please" he said, because he wasn't "going to be no grease monkey for nobody, by God."

One time he was a sample-man for a big soap company. It was his job to give out free samples in neighborhoods of St. Louis and East St. Louis and then, according to an alternating monthly schedule, return to make sales. He was a foreman at the blooming mill by then, but he wanted more. He must have been a very fine sample-man but he was, for certain, no salesman. On every spare inch of the garage floor, tall boxes of WHIM (The Slim Box of Shimmer!) grew pale and bloated from moisture.

In front of the car, on either side of the Snap-On tool chest, were two newspaper Tie-Ups, table machines that grabbed and tied a folded newspaper with a *cashunk!* that was music to Dad's ears during all the time he was a distributor for the *Press Record*. When he lost that job too, I heard him tell her, "Pat, I just can't be a goddamn grown-up paperboy all my life. I just won't!"

So, he did bookkeeping for Gregowizki's Meat Market and some other businesses in Alton and Mitchell. He even had his own office machinery. "He's a smart man," Mother said, earnest in wanting us to believe it. "He's not going to be locked up in the mill all his life, you know."

Around that time, Mom had gone to work in a shoe store. Her one-to-six shift and Dad's combined steel mill grave-yard shift and nine-to-noon work in Alton and Mitchell kept us all apart. Home by ten o'clock, Dad, who had usually been at Mr. Paschowski's since three or four, was a happy drunkard, his strong laughter like the exhalation of pure joy, his inhibitions so uncontained that his love could be as dangerous as his purest anger. Mother became so word-empty that Matthew and I hung on anything she said. At night when she called "Good night" up the stairs to us, that was enough to sleep on. Those two words.

"Love ya guys. 'Night," Dad would call up, much later.

Now, lying back on the Olds, I watched my breath form and dissolve in the cold air. Matthew said, "Maybe Luke could come." He trusted in him more than I did. Sometimes

Luke, who was nineteen then, would come and get us away from the house. He'd drive us somewhere or take us to see the Cards or, in basketball season, the Hawks.

School wasn't working out for him; the coach who recruited him that summer was replaced at the beginning of the semester by a coach who was intent on reassembling at SIU the team he had coached at University of Illinois. I learned a lot later that the new coach was also less interested in education than in what he called "opportunity," which translated to athletic department revenues.

By five o'clock it was already almost dark. "Boys!" she called. Though she knew we were in the garage, she called again louder. I peered through the cracked windows that had been built crookedly into the garage doors. Mud and wind junk had gathered in the glass cracks, and Mother, her hand on one of the porch-swing chains, looked directly at the window but could not see me. "Michael! Matthew!" she called.

One afternoon Matthew and I had watched her and Dad through the garage window. They were sitting together at one end of the swing and rocking it askew each time they pushed off with their feet. Finally, they nudged each other to opposite ends of the swing and pushed off and comfortably swung for half an hour, their locked hands between them.

Now, when she called us again, Matthew mashed his face to the window, making a nose of his tongue and a tongue of his nose. "Okay, Matthew," I said. We pushed open the garage doors.

Inside the house, she asked us to hurry and get washed

up and changed. The sweet smell of the ham made me hungry again, but I didn't ask for any. We changed into better clothes, raked over our hair in the reckless two-stroke we had learned from Dad. She telephoned Grandfather to tell him we were coming.

He must have asked her to reconsider. "Well, we're coming anyway," she answered.

Just before we reached his house, she said, "Grandfather's not in a good mood." I could rarely recall a time when he was. His Lithuanian tradition had taught him women lived to serve men. When Grandmother became ill with heart trouble, the dependencies reversed, and that embittered him.

Though it was windy cold and looked like it might snow, we walked slowly. The Mobil horse had snow on its back and mane, but still turned mightily around and around. Farther on, Stan the Man, his bat blasted with ice, watched. Rounding a corner, we were surprised to see Grandmother a block away, standing on the pitched front yard, waving. She wore a man's old greatcoat and seemed to have difficulty lifting the heavy sleeves of it to move her hand and arm. Like my mother, she was a thin woman. The coat sleeve engulfed her small hand when she stopped waving.

"Hi there!" Matthew called out, waving back. He was undisguisedly her favorite grandchild.

She shifted her weight oddly. Her hand emerged from the coat but didn't take the air as it had before.

"Hi!" Mom called, holding our hands now. "Hi!" she called again. We walked more quickly. Then, Mom said in a whisper, "Mom?"

Grandmother's mouth relaxed into a word she could not

speak. She placed her left foot downhill and reached into the air uphill. Her other hand went to her chest.

"My God!" shouted Mom.

We didn't reach her in time, though for all fifteen yards our feet hardly touched the pavement.

Grandmother's face rested against the top of the pitched yard. Her body lay downhill, the coat covering her like a bank of snow.

Matthew backed away from her. My hand fell out of Mom's. "Grandfather! Grandfather!" I hollered. I pulled him outside. I pointed. When he saw her, he did not leave the porch to go to her, but called her name, "Theresa, Theresa," his voice like a nickel spinning down on a wooden table.

After Grandmother's stroke, Luke dropped by more often. Mom and I and Matthew and Luke visited her. Even Dad sometimes came, but he annoyed my grandfather so much that he seldom stayed long.

At the Christmas family get-together Dad brought Mr. Paschowski to Grandfather's house. The two of them stayed hazardously long. They drank all of Grandfather's wine; Dad was in the mood for celebrating something Luke had privately told him at breakfast.

Mr. Paschowski thanked Grandfather for his (enforced) courtesy. "You are a gracious and thoughtful host indeed!" he said when they came to the last of three bottles. "My own father," he said, "did not know good wines." Saddened, he guzzled. Dad, appreciating Joe's grief, stopped laughing a moment.

Grandmother smiled at them. Except for garbled code,

she had lost the ability to speak, but if she could have, she probably would have remained silent all the same as she watched everyone fawn on Grandfather.

Was he okay alone with her? they wanted to know. "Most times," he answered. Would he like it if they occasionally brought meals? "Could help."

I too found myself keeping a distance between me and the invalid. Polite questions regarding her welfare were safe; we all asked if she was comfortable, if she would like some egg nog or anything, Grandmother. Anything at all, Grandmother? She shook her head. She smiled. If she restrained her emotions, became a kind of machine, she was safe from any more indignities than those already brought on her by her invalidism. If we respected that, treated her like a machine, poured our helpless kind of McWelt love into a more human vessel like Grandfather, were we to blame?

After the get-together was over, the whole group of us said goodbye. Grandmother shut her eyes. We closed her door, wished Grandfather a merry Christmas, told him when we'd next be by to visit. Mom told her sister Norma that she'd watch how Grandfather and Grandmother were getting along and keep her posted until the next weekend. The goodbyes looked to us like they were going to be the usual endless goodbyes, so Luke and Matthew and I went back into Grandmother's room and shut the door behind us.

Her eyes were open. Matthew winked at her.

"Grandmother?" Luke stood apart from her to say it: "I love you, Grandmother." When he came to her bedside, she grimaced, closed her eyes. Despite that, he kissed her cheek. "It's not fair," he said.

On the walk home, Mom was too talkative. The way she always was before a fight. She acted like she hadn't even noticed Dad and Mr. Paschowski's behavior. She told me about how Grandmother had always loved roses. I asked why Grandmother had never grown any, and she answered that she had never had the time.

"Damn right about that!" my dad broke in. "When did your pop give her time?"

"Shush, my dear fellow," said Mr. Paschowski.

Mom glared. "But I'm going to make her a quilt," she said to me, "with roses the size of cantaloupes on it."

When we got home there was a fight. I walked with Mr. Paschowski across the backyard to make sure he got home safely. I sat in the garage until it was over, wondering if Luke and Matthew were going to come out to be with me. Always the one who put in the last word, Dad said loudly enough to be heard a block away, "It's my day off, by God, and I've got it coming."

It was quiet a long while. The cold weather had frozen the tall boxes of WHIM into odd shapes.

"Michael!" my mother called.

"Hey, Mike," Luke said, "it's okay."

I stayed in the garage.

Dad eventually tramped out of the house and across the alley to Mr. Paschowski's. Luke and Matthew came outside. They brought me into the house where we silently watched television. Two hours later, we had still hardly spoken, when Luke broke the news. He said to Mom, "Homer Teppel says I'll be able to get on at the mill right away."

She said, "You didn't tell us—your scholarship—what

did you think—what were you thinking of—all at once like this." She lowered her face. "All—everything at once."

After she left the room, I started to say something to him. Matthew beat me to it. "How about we go get him?"

"Huh?" I said.

"What?" Luke said, then, "Sure. What a great stupid idea, Matthew."

We had never gone into Mr. Paschowski's house. We knocked loudly. Opening the door, Dad said, "Quit the racket. The judge is asleep in his chambers. Come on in." He lowered himself to the floor and sat with his bottle propped on his knees. He pointed with his thumb to the room where Mr. Paschowski was. "Fast asleep."

We went inside to check on him, and found him lying in perfect grinning contentment on one of the only three pieces of furniture in his entire house, the kitchen table. "Does he have a bed?" I asked. In the next room, Dad's laughter was frail.

"Well?" Luke said.

"Ell," he said, "is a hole in the ground."

"He *had* a whole house full of nice—"

"Booze," said Dad. "And a TV."

Matthew said, "Boy. Look."

"He had nice things," I said. I was sure.

"Never." We walked into Mr. Paschowski's small bed-room and then into each empty room. "All ays this ay, boys."

"Not funny," said Luke.

I strained to remember a sofa. A chair. We sat on the floor near Dad.

"And a judge too . . . the successfulest." He said it to

Luke. I could see that this was justice as Dad perceived it: even the mighty college-educated have nothing in the end. What is there to envy?

We watched while he finished his bottle of bourbon, sharing with Luke.

"Last of the good stuff," he said finally. He took up Luke's hand. "Here's to the future."

"Yeah," said Luke.

"Go on, you two," Dad said to Matthew and me, "she's going to be in flames."

We walked out through Mr. Paschowski's back door. The neon lit a word at a time of the faraway Baseball Cardinal's billboard high up on the bridge. We followed the cue and together we mimicked Harry Carey: "It's—A—Home— Run!!!"

I can pull my knees up—right now I can pull them up and cradle my head on the quilt my mother took twelve years to make, and, I tell you, I remember everything.

Later that night, after Mom had gone to sleep, we heard Luke and Dad talking more and more loudly on the back porch. Matthew said we shouldn't, but I called him a chicken if he wouldn't put pants and coat on and go out to the porch with me. I was afraid to go out there alone.

Trying an imitation of Mr. Paschowski, Luke said, "We have company, do we not? Two young candidates for the priesthood."

Dad said, "Son, bring me that red bottle. That one there."

Matthew brought him the red bottle and another one from their places behind the porch swing where Luke and

Dad sat. Dad took the bottles in hand and asked us to "sit up here ith us, boys."

The collars up on our coats, we fitted ourselves on the porch swing, me to Dad's left, Matthew on Luke's right. We pushed off, and rocked unevenly.

Luke pointed to the Mobil horse, pale and chipped, moving slowly but still powerfully. Dad looked too.

We could see our four breaths. We couldn't—none of us could find the porch floor with our feet and, so, we couldn't push off again. Through the twisted white air I saw the world drunkenly pitch and ripple.

"Whoa!" said Dad.

Steeper and steeper, everything arched before us. I imagined I saw Mom waving her hand from atop it. It all became—the whole arching world converging at a single place, like the Gateway to the West—like the mound that covers a freshly dug grave.

"Whoa!" said Dad, laughing.

"Whoa!" we said. We all said it. We all laughed. I was only twelve, but it occurred to me that our laughter was very old.

Eventually, we stopped rocking, dizzy and giddy. "You boys all right?" Dad asked, "Hoop? Hoop, you all right now?"

Answering for him, Matthew said, "Underful! Underful!"

When Luke McWelt first considered stopping his hobo's life he wasn't exactly sure why. It might have been his brother Michael or Michael's wife. Or Clair, their two-year-old daughter. It might have been the bicycle lady's first appearance. For a long time before any of it, he had felt his comfortable solitude become expectant. And then, he was sure things began to change the first week in December. A Friday.

Luke sized up the Friday lunch-break group in front of Bogel's Deli and he knew only his best trick would do. Because of the cold, the audience was quieter; a few men mumbled above the whirr of the hot whipped cocoa machine but traffic and the ring of Bogel's cash register blurred their voices. Luke stood with the Sierra de la Soledad to his back. To the west an arm of the Rio Grande was protectively crooked around the winter-stilled pecan orchards and the chile and cotton farms around Mesilla. In the air he could smell steaming cocoa and coffee and the odors of Las Almas: the seeds of the yucca and the fine blonde dust from the dry fields and the grit from the streets, all shaken into and just as instantly waved from the air by the stiff winds; the rusting of steel and the wearing away of straw-sweet adobe; the waste of horses and cattle and the exhaust of pickups.

Luke relaxed his shoulders and knees. Everything was perfect. His shoes were untied. His sweater was buttoned unevenly. Because he knew folks liked a happy hobo best, he smiled his mouth-agape smile. He might watch their eyes, but he never made direct eye contact with anyone. That would be cruel.

If he wanted to take a chance, he could do his new trick, the one with two baseball bats, a jersey, and a Cardinal's cap. But he knew it was a cheat-and-a-trick really. The cap's bill was cloth-covered tin, and it drilled the sky like a grackle.

It wasn't the right day for a cheat-and-a-trick. The businessmen's shirtsleeves were rolled down, their ties were straight and tight, their belts cinched. Two of his friends from the Gospel Rescue Mission were there. Jerry held his white Bible as if it were buttered bread he would offer someone any second. Katherine Arrowen held Jerry in check because she respected Luke's turf. She and Luke had gotten involved once. Now that he lived apart from the Rescue Mission regulars, he was an outsider there also, even to Katherine.

He glanced past Katherine's face. A dark Chicana in an overlarge red turtleneck sweater parked her bicycle and waited, watched. She held a small cloth bag on the bicycle crossbar.

A bike, for Christ's sake. It made Luke smile more broadly. He wondered how the crowd regarded her, and, for a moment, he was tempted to look in their faces to find out. He had shaken their hands; knew their names; except for the woman, he had seen all of them before. For years, he was sure some of them had given as much money to him as to their children's weekly allowances or their church collections or office charities. Still, he had never looked into their eyes. It was the single most saddening drawback in his nine years of hobo life.

Okay then, he said to himself. All right. The Voit trick. He pulled his basketball out of the box behind him. He palmed it in his left hand, held it over his head and poised himself exactly like a trophy, on his toes. "Hello," he said, relaxing only a little.

"From my height, you might have guessed I played some basketball once." He wondered who could imagine a hobo as ever anything more than a hobo. Even he could hardly imagine himself as the best center in the history of the Meltenville Magicians. But he was. The Meltenville salutatorian, too. "A shy prize," his mother had said, "my shy prize." Luke "the Hoop" McWelt, the pride of southern Illinois high school basketball.

"The team," he said to the businessmen, "the team I played for called me Hoop." He stretched himself to his full six feet seven inches. He lowered his arm and caressed the dimples, which he called "buds," on the surface of the ball.

"I played pretty good," he said. They had just started to listen. He had played better than pretty good, as a matter of fact. Now, almost forty, he was standing in front of a deli in Las Almas, New Mexico, doing tricks with a basketball.

"Now *this*," he said, spinning the ball, "is the Voit." Though most of them knew the Voit rap by heart, they attentively listened. He often imagined them delivering the Voit rap to their children: "Now this. . . ." He saw the woman lean against her bike, listening with head-bent concentration. Her slight open smile was knowing, confident in a way that made him uneasy. Her lips brightened as they pressed together, defining faint lines at her cheeks and chin. He guessed her age as late thirties.

"The Voit—," he spun the ball from one hand to another, "is a technical achievement great as a great dam or a spaceship." He raised his left knee and spun the ball there, bumped it up and gyroscoped it over his right arm, shoulders, and left arm. He steadily dribbled it left-handed. "A wonder," he said, respectfully studying the jackhammering bounce of it. Accelerating the ball's force by alternately punching it with his closed fists, he searched for a watch on someone near him so he could time himself (he knew this audience would not stay for a trick more than ten minutes long).

"The black seams," Luke said, affecting a calm tape-recorded museum voice, "are like longitudes." He palmed the ball and turned it. "Or latitudes." He wondered why his brother Michael, standing a little apart from the crowd, had come again, his tired eyes averted, his large hands locked into fists.

Luke dropped the ball, dribbled it very low with his right hand, now with his right foot, then his left foot, then his left hand. *Fabumabumabumabum!* He wished Michael hadn't come.

"The Voit," he said, "has eight continents, each populated by three thousand, three hundred and thirty-four buds."

With the point of his right elbow he spiked the ball into the air. *Fabum!* And with his left elbow again—*Fabum!*—this time several feet above his head.

From the cardboard box in back of him he pulled out a simple pine yardstick. He baton-twirled it in his right hand. He held inch one in his fingertips.

A few people were laughing. Some were already anticipating the next part of the rap; their lips formed the words *Who knows. . . .* Everyone watched him. (He considered whether or not he liked them—Mr. Bogel, Mr. Fortham the funeral director, Dr. Telles the university professor, the rest—and he wished he could know just that one thing.) Freeing his loose-jawed bum's smile, Luke said, "Who knows how many total buds on a Voit?"

All the regulars knew; all of them probably mentally rehearsed the number. But they wouldn't say it. They were serious men, after all, these men, and no trick on earth could change that. "Okay," Luke said, always careful not to press them. Once more, he pounded the ball into the cold air high above him. Timing was everything. "Who knows how many buds?"

He pinched the very end of the yardstick, holding inch one between his thumb and forefinger. When the ball sank, he caught it on inch thirty-six and balanced it there. "Twenty-six thousand—"

"Six hundred and seventy-two buds," said the bicycle lady.

It had never happened. Luke almost dropped the Voit. "And—and—Valve, King of the Buds!" he said. He pointed to the valve at the vortex of the spinning basketball.

He tried to but could not avoid her eyes. *Fabum!* He sent it up again. Undistracted by the ball landing perfectly on the yardstick end, she stared. He shook his head, smiled at her, and concentrated again on the trick.

Crouching like a catcher, he bounced the ball onto inch thirty-three at the end of the yardstick and began to dribble it toward him. It rhythmically hit the top of the stick. It accelerated. *Futuhtuhtuhtuhtuh.*

When he did this part of the trick, everyone always stopped eating. When he did this part of the trick, it was so quiet he sometimes thought they stopped breathing. *Futuhtuhtuhtuhtuh.* The ball moved further down the yardstick. The movements of his wrist were so slight they were imperceptible. Their silence opened their thoughts to him; they wondered: Are both the yardstick and the ball moving? How? Where is the trick—in the ball or in the stick? What kind of a hobo is this?

Luke glanced at Michael, whose liquor-blank face shirked into the raised collar of his coat. The bicycle lady had crossed her arms over her small breasts and she breathed unevenly. She appeared to be trying to multiply it all—the crowd, the silence, the trick, the bum—into a total. She had stopped staring. She watched the ball.

Now he dribbled the Voit up each inch of the yardstick until it reached his wrist. He threw the ball from his wrist almost fifteen feet into the air, caught and balanced it at inch thirty-six, turned it over and, once more using the yardstick end, he dribbled it low against the pavement. *Futuhbumatuhbumatubum. Futuhbumatuhbumatuhbumatuhbum!* High above his head now.

He caught it on the quarter-inch end of the perpendicular yardstick. He spun and balanced it there. He sent it up once more. A little higher than believable. They didn't believe, he knew. He sent it a little higher. Past disbelief. It stayed in the air. Stayed and stayed and stayed and missiled downward and arrived faster than doubt.

It hit the quarter-inch end of the perpendicular yardstick once more. Once more he spun and balanced it there. He should remember to look goofy (they liked it if he looked a little goofy for this part) but he didn't want to. *Boom!* He banged it against the pavement as if to send it out of the reach of even dream. But he stopped it cold, deadened it on the stick, blew his warm white breath on it.

"Like a great dam," he said. "Or a spaceship." He let it spin down, tipped the stick horizontally, balanced the perfectly still ball at the end. "The Voit," he said quietly, prayerfully. "The Voit." He lowered it to the ground.

Reaching behind him, he found his coffee cup and, placing it on the yardstick, he passed it around. "Thank you," he said. "Thanks so much." The woman had disappeared.

Michael emerged a little from his coat, stepping forward only when the crowd was completely gone. Luke put the cup and ball and stick into his cardboard box and picked it up.

"Luke?" Michael said, as if not recognizing him.

"Why do you come?"

Michael pulled at the collar of his coat. "I don't know."

Behind Michael, Katherine Arrowen waved, said, "See you, Luke," and strode away with Jerry in tow. "God bless!" said Jerry, probably in anger more than in benediction.

"I'll come by," Luke called to them. He asked Michael, "Well, what did you think?"

"Will you come by the house, Luke?"

"What did you think?"

"I didn't look."

Luke went into the old Conoco service station that was now Bogel's Deli. He thanked the old man's son, Dave Bogel, who said, "You're what brings 'em, I swear."

"Ain't I though?" Luke turned around to introduce Michael, but his brother was staring through the front windows where Bogel had stenciled, ASK ABOUT THE LUNCH SPECIAL and COME INSIDE!

They walked the eight blocks past the Hidden Forrest restaurant and bar and the Villa Motel to the El Don Motel, behind which Michael and Ruth's trailer was parked. Ruth had been a photojournalist but managed the El Don now.

Michael opened the door for Luke and took his box. He set it on the stoop outside. "That *is* some trick," he said.

"Illusion, Michael." Luke took the Voit from him.

Over lunch, Luke watched for the change in his brother. Ruth and the child, Clair, seemed to be waiting also.

Friday was Michael's only day off from stocking and clerking at the office supply store, his only night off from the Camino Vista Bowling Lanes, where he was the janitor on the midnight-to-eight shift. It always took a while—it often took a full bottle of scotch—before he could "unwind," as he put it. And when Michael was tense, his jaw a lock and his gray eyes alert, thin basketball player's chest expanded and the calves of his long legs pressed against his chair, he had the same almost childlike appearance that Luke recognized in himself and remembered in their father. He had slight ankles and slight wrists, though each open hand measured about nine inches from the tip of his little finger to his thumbnail. He had the McWelt brown hair, fine, dark, but light at the temples and sideburns so his face always had the expression of a child inside a man inside a child. For the same reason, their father, a resolute alcoholic who "unwound," he said, "in shifts," had never fully shown the toll of his twenty-four years of sixty-hour work weeks.

The flautas Ruth made were fat with carne adobada and smothered with homemade guacamole, but as a point of pride, Luke ate little. He was never really hungry. Often he gave some of his food to hobos in Las Almas, most of them from Juarez, across the border. On the Fridays that the weather kept him from performing a trick and on the holidays that the businessmen stayed home, he usually had enough canned food stored away to get by. He sometimes thought that if he didn't watch himself he could, in fact, become fat. In

March and April, wild asparagus grew everywhere along the irrigation ditches. In May and June the Mesilla Valley always produced more onions than the migrant workers could take from the fields. Green chiles spilled from brimming trucks July through September. Then, in early October, the dry red chiles were ready, and the twenty thousand acres of pecan trees along Highway 28 bowed down and invited thieves to unburden them. In the 1930s the Mesilla Valley had been the hobos' Eden. Luke, who still had an athlete's concern for his physical condition, never took more than he would need or could give away. Besides, he always thought, people suspect an overweight hobo.

Clair gurgled, pushing her food from her mouth onto her chin. She looked through Luke with her messy smile.

Wiping her chin and neck, Luke asked, "Is she done?"

"Very," said Ruth. She unfastened the high chair tray and lifted Clair into Michael's arms, telling her something in the Tewa language. Closing her hands around the pens in his shirt pocket, the child gave Michael a kiss on the chest, leaving a trace of green food on his shirt. She held two ink pens to her stomach.

Michael kissed her ticklish neck; he held her head in his hands and whispered something musical into her ear. He leaned back from her and asked, "Okay?"

She giggled, looking at her mother, who shrugged and asked the child a long question in Tewa. Clair slowly shook her head. She put the pens back.

"Jesus," said Luke. It always amazed him how the child completely understood Ruth, could understand so much though able to speak only fragmented sentences. But that was Ruth's doing. From the first time he met her, Luke had been confused by Ruth Walalata because she made him doubt everything he thought he knew about faith. She was Indian, but not Indian. She had confronted, accepted, rejected, and reshaped in herself the traditions that have everything to do with culture and, finally, absolutely nothing to do with it. It wasn't Tewa that Ruth nourished in Clair and it wasn't Anglo either; it was moment-to-moment reinvention. She had said it once: "To hear a bell ringing and make a bell and steeple and bellringer in your head—it's ignorant and a shame to do that." In Ruth's way of thinking, Clair was not Tewa, but her own pure, undirected, undirectable note. And Ruth was that herself.

Michael ruffled Clair's fine black hair with his nose. He whispered into her ear again, and again he leaned back. "Okay," he said. He grinned at her. Luke caught his eye, and Michael smiled but lowered his head as if to keep his pride secret. He passed Clair to Luke.

When Michael returned from the kitchen, he carried a whiskey and water, already half empty. Luke said, "Okay? Okay, Clair?"

"Okay," said the child.

Together, the men lifted and tumbled Clair and gingerly passed her back and forth. Crawling after her to the living room of the trailer, they sat her on the floor between them and played a game Luke had devised called Try This One On. He touched his hand to her forehead, arched his arm dramatically and announced, "A one-plume forehead hat!" Michael finished his drink. He added his hand and arm to Luke's and imitated him. "A two-plume forehead hat!"

"But not quite you, Clair," said Luke with the serious affectation of a high-tone salesman.

"No. Course not," said Michael, his words slurred a little. Their mock-serious expressions delighted her. "She needs her a—a what? A low-slung two-headed holster!" Each lightly pressed the top of his head into her side. Even Ruth's closed smile broke.

For almost half an hour they nudged Clair, rocked her, flew her into and out of each other's arms with the grace that distinguished them as McWelts. No three brothers ever handled a basketball like the McWelt brothers, Luke, Michael, and Matthew. Talk of the town in season and out. Meltenville's claim to fame.

Exhausted, the two men finally lay on their backs and let Clair crawl over them, tug at their hair, and pull on their lips and ears. "What a kid," said Luke. His brother, staring at the ceiling, said, "Sure loves her uncle."

Luke wondered why they had never been able to say it to each other: to say that they loved each other in some way other than by code. In one-on-one basketball the chummy slaps had meant that; in church, the conspiratorial wise-guy nods had meant that; as adults, the bitching about jobs. And Matthew, whom they had lost—they had meant to say how much they loved him, loved each other. Why hadn't they? Because there was always a way to avoid it.

Clair crawled to her mother and sat quietly, listening to a melody Ruth hummed.

"Luke," Michael said. "You found a job?"

Michael knew better. "I'm not looking," Luke said. "I've told you before—"

"You're happy. I know. I know. You're happy bumming off people on a street corner."

Luke sat up. The argument had been constant since the first day Michael arrived in Las Almas from Illinois. Luke was tired of arguing. "I'm a good 'bo," he said. "I'm happy."

Michael raised himself to his full height and stood over Luke. The booze had finally steadied him. He was unwound. He kicked Luke very lightly. "Luke-the-bum-happy-Hoop." As quickly as always, the argument was over.

"It's awful outside," said Michael who could never stay *inside* anywhere without getting restless.

Luke grinned at him. "If you were a playing card your face wouldn't be worth five points, Michael."

"So?"

"Come on."

They walked outside in the sharp winter air. Even far from the trailer, they heard Ruth's soft music, an eerie imitation of surf. "Hay–ay ay ya a a–a–h oh o way–ay . . ." Ruth had told him it was a Tewa creation song.

Luke said, "Cold and bright."

"No snow here in the valley," Michael said. He shrugged his shoulders toward the white-capped mountain peaks.

"No."

"You're not. I mean—a bum."

"No."

"Not *that* kind, Luke." He turned his head into the strong wind, and the cold dulled his eyes.

"Can I come next Friday?" Luke asked.

Michael smiled his daughter's unreserved smile. The unclosed curves of his love were conveyed in it and in the lines around his mouth. He nodded for them to go back.

"Thanks," Luke said. At the door, he picked up the box and waved goodbye to Clair and Ruth. "Bye, Ruth. Thanks."

"Luke, come back, okay?" she said. She raised Clair's hand and Clair waved. For the time and money needed to care for Clair and Michael, Ruth had quit her job as photographer at the *Sun-Bulletin* and sold her cameras and, eventually, her darkroom equipment.

Luke started to say more to her but, instead, returned to kiss Clair and make a last great pretend-hat on her head.

The walk to the hut on the Rio Grande was long. He could have asked for a ride, but he did not want to risk letting Michael see his home. He walked almost a straight line south from the trailer, then he crossed the railroad tracks into Mesilla and, taking a shortcut through the unfenced edges of two chile farms, he walked past the Mesilla Co-Op Gin, a kind of corrugated steel cardhouse surrounded by a ghostly herd of large wooden trailers and flatbeds. The gin always reminded him of the Meltenville steel mill.

Like his brothers, Luke had proven himself back home. He and Matthew had been stars in basketball, and Michael a first-squad player in several sports. They had proven themselves in the classroom too, pushing from one level of learning to another as if they were learning new moves on the court. Each brother had earned scholarships generous enough to assure him a college education, a ticket out of Meltenville, but ended up staying home to work at the steel mill.

Then, their dad died from injuries in a car accident on his way home from the midnight shift. After ten years at the blast furnace, Luke simply quit, and, on short notice, said goodbye to everyone. A job with a bakery was waiting for him in New Mexico, he said. Michael and Matthew argued that it was senseless; they asked him what he was going to do with himself in a land of dust and bones and dusty, bony people. But he knew they envied him. Their mother, on the other hand, had religion, and she could see that Luke's decision was a "part of God's plan for our family."

Luke laughed, held the small woman in his arms, asked her to forget it. "Mom," he said, "it's all the stations with you, isn't it? Fourteen stations: one worse than the other, right up to the moment of salvation."

That was eleven years ago. Now, Matthew was dead. And Michael's alcoholism was far worse since he, too, had come out to New Mexico.

As Luke walked through a blighted arbor of young, shoulder-high pecan trees and came within sight of his hut under Black Mesa, he tiptoed past old lady Romelia's bee boxes along the ditch banks. He crossed the dry plank bridge. What station, he wondered, is this?

2

Eight in the morning on Saturday. I woke up needing to go to the john. On the sofa across the room, Matthew lay with his long legs dangling over one armrest, his arms flung up and over his head. He looked like he was in a fade-away jumpshot. "In!" I said. I went back to sleep but couldn't get b-ball off my mind.

Luke was called "Luke the Hoop" in Meltenville. Still is, I bet. He was that good. I guess because Matthew and I were expected to be that good we were too. Matthew averaged twenty-three points a game—six more than Luke's average—for his three years of high school basketball, but no one gave him the honor of a nickname.

"McWelt! McWelt! McWelt!" the fans and players hollered at Matthew on downcourt drives and scrambles under the boards. What I mean to say is they hollered it *at* him. He *should* shoot: it was a demand, not just a hope. When Matthew took to the air and line-drived the ball from the sidecourt into the basket, you almost couldn't believe it whipped into and out of the strings so hard, so rapid-fire. "McWelt! McWelt! McWelt!" they shouted, and backslapped and bumped each other, as many as five thousand people some nights. People knew my brothers' names from

Collinsville to Alton to Belleville to Wood River to East St. Louis.

Luke had a high, dramatic arcing shot. "Hoop! Hoop! Hoop!" they screamed at him. But when he sent the ball way high over all our heads, way impossibly high over the basket, the auditorium became so silent you could hear the holy swishing sound of the strings barely kissed by the ball.

So, for Matthew, lots of honor. But no nickname.

At about nine o'clock I was just out of the shower when Matthew woke up. I heard him grunt. "Okay?" I said.

"Legs fell asleep," he said.

"Ought to take your shoes off when you go to sleep, Matthew."

"Yeah." He toyed with the few dark hairs on his chin. Darker than the long dark brown hair on his head, they made him look like some kind of goat or buffalo or something.

"Like to shoot some baskets when you come back to life?"

He said, "There's snow on the ground!"

"Not much on the courts."

"Ice, anyway."

"Okay," I said, though I wanted to play real bad. I offered him a beer, which he took into the shower with him. I set mine on the bathroom sink. "Quit using so much hot water," I said. "I can't see my damn face to shave."

"So shave something else."

I turned the hot water on full in the sink in order to freeze him in the shower.

"Hey!" he said.

I chanted, "McWelt! McWelt! McWelt!" When I knew he'd turned the hot water all the way up in the shower, I turned it off in the sink.

"Hey!"

"McWelt! McWelt! McWelt!" I hollered.

He gave in.

"Just a few games of long-and-short," I promised.

We put sweatpants and jackets on and walked to the hoops behind St. Elizabeth's Hospital. A surgeon in town who knew more about healing than other doctors had paid for the hoops to be put up in 1960, and the hospital staff replaced the hoop chains every April whether they needed replacing or not.

We'd gotten a letter from Luke on Wednesday or Thursday and we talked about that. Las Almas was booming, he wrote. He had been keeping an eye on the sign painting competition, like always, and it was still small potatoes. "But you'd better come quick," his letter said. "Las Almas *must* need signs and bigger ones too. Hell, you can still see the mountains!"

Matthew concentrated on his set shot. "You just can't help loving the bum," he said, and pumped the shot in.

"Not funny," I said because I didn't think it was one bit funny to have my older brother bumming for a living.

Matthew rebounded. "Well, bum or not, you can't help it." His short shot circled the rim. "Can you?"

"No. I guess not." It had been about four years since we'd seen him. We figured from his letters he must be a damn good bum. ("Hobo," he called himself.) Never unhappy in a single line, he wrote us letters that were like little gifts, telling us how great a place it was, dreamily describing everything we dreamed of New Mexico being. Enchant-mentland.

He always started out an exaggeration with, "I'd be lying if I didn't tell you. . . ."

"I'd be lying if I didn't tell you the dust storms march across here like legions of demons." "I'd be lying if I didn't tell you the ocotillo and yuccas and red chiles smell a little better than perfumed nightgowns." Anyway, we figured that anyone who could float shots in from the head of the key like Luke had, and fib in letters like he could, must make a good bum.

It was nice talking about the desert as we blew on our frozen fingers and skidded over the icy pavement on our way back to the apartment. While we were changing into our work clothes, Russo, the day foreman, called and said Homer had told him we *wanted* our butts fried in the smokestack. "Can you believe that guy?" he said. I was glad we were on the phone because in person he had a way of putting his face close to you and rummaging inside you. If we were really that stupid, he said, we should wait until four to come in; by then the slab ovens at the hot strip would have been down for eight hours and it'd be safer to start.

We went to Marco's for some catfish sandwiches and cold beer. We talked about how Marco made the business go.

"What is this place?" Matthew asked. He answered him-self, "It's a shack with some fryers and an icebox."

"And a cash register."

"Yeah," he said, disappointed in my priorities.

"And the whole Marco family working for nothing."

"Yeah," he said, "but buying straight teeth and compact cars and college educations."

We bought more beer, which was cheaper in Marco's than anywhere else. The big dill pickles were free but if you took too many, one of the Marcowitz sisters told on you, and one of the brothers said something to one of the cousins, who came to your table and said, "Zaduzo," which meant, "Too many."

At about two o'clock, we left for You Dam Right. The fly ash from the mill darkened the falling snow so that at night you could never find the moon except in the glittering, steely flakes. I wish I knew how to distill the matchhead taste on our tongues; it made you say, "To hell with the moon—who needs the moon?" because you had the blaze of the molten pig iron carried in metal cars to the basic oxygen furnace, and you had the ingots thundering helplessly against compression at the blooming mill and screaming in the hot strip as four-ton slabs heated at 2300 degrees before they were tortured through rollers into a sixteenth of an inch of hissing steel. It made you want to shout, "Match that heat, God! Match a goddamn sixteenth of an inch!"

Four thousand people worked in that steel mill where the smokestacks had coughed fly ash for eighty years over the sand prairie land called the American Bottoms, once so famous for high-acre yield that I bet the farmers used to dare God, too.

Matthew asked me what I was thinking.

I belched. "Zaduzo!"

We asked Knud to serve us anything that thawed fingers and faces.

"So?" he said. "What'd you want?"

Matthew made a frown of concentration into a grin. "Tequila."

"Got some?" I asked.

"Somewhere." His sister Edna was helping him tend bar. We heard him ask her about it. When he came back with it, we bought the bottle.

What did Knud look like? I want to remember.

•

The hut was tucked against the small bluff of Black Mesa called El Cerro. It fronted the Rio Grande and was almost hidden by high reeds and the westernmost reach of Stahmann's pecan orchards. A hole broken in the adobe served as a back window. The front door was narrow and the frame low. He ducked under it, pulling his box inside. He flinched. "What the—Sovel?" The last people on earth Luke wanted to see were Sovel and Sovel's brother-in-law, Marvin.

Sovel, still sitting, pushed his head forward and extended his hand into the faint shaft of moonlight separating them. "What you think—am I still the handsomest dog you seen in two years? Is it been two years?"

Luke didn't know. It hadn't been long enough.

"Hi," Marvin said, lamely shaking Luke's hand. "Missed you," he said. He meant it. Marvin always meant what he said. And Marvin had always looked—Luke almost couldn't name it—ill. For years he had talked of a spur, low in the back of his head, that "gets my brains galloping." He was about forty, and at least twenty years younger than Sovel, but looked the older. Sovel's sparse, graying red hair was brushed from his left ear to his right and then back so that it all bunched on that one side of his head. Marvin, a large-framed man a little taller than Luke, was even thinner than he had been two years ago.

"What the hell are you doing here?" Luke asked.

"We got a job," said Marvin.

Sovel withdrew his head from the light. "Right."

It wasn't like Sovel to be brief. Luke knew it was unwise to tempt him to say more. But Marvin and Sovel were hobos, professional hobos almost all their lives, and he was too curious not to ask it. "Here?"

"Dishwashers," Sovel said. "Albuquerque."

"You? Dishwashers?"

Receiving some kind of signal from Sovel, Marvin hesitated. "In a cafeteria. The university there's got a big one."

Luke was thankful they were just dropping by because when they stayed they stayed forever. They usually left only after the problems they had caused him began to inconvenience them also. "So, why are you here?"

"Not your working kind, if you get me. We quit." Sovel stretched himself out on the narrow strip of carpet that was Luke's bed. He unbuttoned the army-green greatcoat he was wearing and pulled it closer around him.

Luke asked, "But you're going back, right? You're not staying around here? You're *not* staying around here, Sovel."

"Hoop, what I say is there's no friends like *no* friends. People just smell in general and stink in particular." Sovel spat on the dirt floor of the hut. He wiped his chin clean. "And, Hoop, me and him're just awful tired of people."

"Except for you, Luke," said Marvin innocently. Marvin wasn't sitting right; his body leaned away from his head and neck.

"God help me," Luke said.

Sovel tucked his hands under his wide buttocks and rocked himself on his palms. "Marvin, you okay?"

"Uh-huh," said Marvin, "I think." He rose awkwardly, tried to sit next to Luke, but still could not sit right. "Did you ever figure out the trick with the yardstick and the basketball?"

"Yeah," said Sovel, "What come a that?"

Luke could not help talking to them; that was the penalty of his solitude. And, because it plainly would not matter to Sovel if he was rude or friendly, he decided to be civil. For Marvin's sake. But only for a little while. Ignoring Sovel, he said, "The problem was with the balls I was using, not the stick."

"Always is," said Sovel. "Always is the balls." He laughed up another spit.

"Spit outside, huh?" said Luke.

Sovel swallowed it. He nodded to Marvin. "He don't get it."

Marvin, who always smiled when Sovel indicated he should, said, "Oh," and tried to smile. "What kind of balls do you use?" Marvin asked.

Luke could put some one part of Marvin aside—the eagerness in the set of his broad shoulders, the indisturbable trust in his gaze—but the whole of him was a gentle welcome he could not turn from. "It's a Voit," he said. Marvin looked confused. "You have to have a Voit, Marvin. And you have to fill it way too full."

"You can do it now?" Marvin asked.

"Sure. I had the Voit all along and didn't use it." He hoped that was the end of it. He stepped outside. "Shit, you guys, this is a bad time," he said. He said it louder. "This is a bad time to be coming here to suck me dry."

No word came from his hut. "Did you hear me, Sovel?"

"We heard. Come in out a the cold, Luke."

"Shit." Luke walked away, heading upriver.

He sat down against a bare mesquite tree a trumpet vine had overtaken. If he waited them out maybe they would just rob him of his canned goods and clothes and go on their way.

He gave them an hour. Then he walked back very slowly. He passed the old lady Romelia's adobe three-room, which apparently had once been painted bright sky blue but now was only vaguely stained. In the two small windows on either side of her door were dolls wearing bright orange and yellow and fiesta-colored hoop skirts. All the dolls faced inward. Still, Luke admired their necks and the backs of their dark arms. Once a month he delivered Romelia's honey to Albertson's Market, where Mr. Zoeller charged customers too much for it but sold every jar and traded Romelia groceries, asking her nothing extra against her profits. Though he didn't see Romelia inside now, Luke waved as he passed because she was in there somewhere. She never left.

In the hut, Marvin lay on his side with his neck arched and his forehead pressed into the dirt floor. Sovel, his eyes closed, still rocked himself on his palms. Luke knew he should make them go.

In the years since their last visit, Sovel was unchanged. A little less harsh with Marvin than before but still a bully. He was one of the only hobos Luke had ever met who could pitifully ask, "You maybe got spare change for my son here?"

and point at Marvin (who would be doing his Eager Retard act) and, receiving nothing, angrily demand, "What kind a human awr you?" And be given money! And then, accusing the person with his eyes, he'd say, "Thank you!" like, "About time!"

Now, whether Luke wanted it or not, Sovel had invited himself and Marvin to stay and there would be no way to avoid it. Luke said, "You inviting yourself to stay the night?"

Sovel didn't answer.

Marvin shifted into a position that looked even less comfortable. "Please?" he asked.

"You've got plans?" Luke asked.

Sovel said, "Plans?" He creased the collar of his gray cotton work shirt between his index fingers and thumbs and then stroked his neck with great self-affection. "Laid and ready to hatch, you could say."

"Marvin?"

"Right, Luke."

"Kinda the plan to end all plans," said Sovel.

"Right, Luke."

Luke shook his head. "*Big* trouble, in other words?"

"No trouble at all."

"Honest," said Marvin, his lead-blue eyes pleading.

"Put us up, then?" Sovel asked.

"Sure." I'll be sorry, Luke thought. "Sure, Marvin." He couldn't help liking Marvin. "And if you guys leave in a month," he said, "I'll be lucky, won't I?"

Speaking into the ground, Marvin said, "Thanks."

As he had all his adult life, Luke slept hard for about two hours and woke and caught only moments of rest from then until morning. The steel mill shift work of three generations of McWelt men was in his blood; he slept this way because his dreams were only the length of certain tasks. In them, he shouted in order to be heard above the din of machinery. When he woke, unable to breathe, his neck glistening with sweat, he knew it was from the close heat of gray-red ingots and the smothering dust of cooling steel sheets gliding overhead on magnetic cranes.

Now, early in the morning, a thousand miles from all that, he thought of Matthew, who had died in one of the giant smokestacks that rose out of the slab ovens into a sky darkened with gases and dusts. He had never heard of it, sending someone into those stacks. What was the point? Who decides those jobs, pencils them down on those time sheets and never once thinks about more than the production schedule?

He turned to face the pitted adobe wall. When he closed his eyes again, he dreamed himself doing his trick. "The Voit," he was saying, "is a technical. . . ." From the tip of the yardstick, he slapped the ball high overhead. As it plummeted down out of the New Mexico sky, he forgot. "Is a technical achievement . . . a . . . is a technical achievement. . . ." For a moment, the helpless fear he had often known in the steel mill bound him. He could not catch his breath.

Then, the two thin brown arms of the Chicana encircled his waist; from behind him he heard the word *great* whispered; the warm corner of her lips touched his left ear. "Great," she said. The Voit hit the yardstick and stayed.

"A technical achievement—great—great as a great dam or spaceship," he announced.

He sat up and crossed his sweat-soaked arms, chilled by

the cold air in the hut. Though it was already getting light, he decided to build a small fire and he went outside for wood.

Returning with some scraps, he noticed that Sovel's eyes were open. His stare was threatening.

"Sovel," he whispered. "What's up?"

"Hoop," Sovel said. "You wouldn't buy it."

"Buy what?"

Sovel brought his elbows closer together so that he was looking through the narrow channel of his arms. "Hoop, he's really sick."

"Huh?"

"Marvin."

"Sure," said Luke, who knew, after all, that Marvin *was* sick, though never as sick as he seemed. It was like Sovel to con even the people who knew his cons by heart.

Luke placed the kindling in a dug-out corner of the hut and lit the scraps with a cap of kerosene from a can near Sovel's feet. He sat down across from the fire. "Jesus, Sovel. What do you take me for?"

"Really, Hoop. He's bad," Sovel whispered. "Tumor, way back there. Maybe growing." His oily hair and the unwashed skin of his face reflected the fire's first high flames. "Worse and worse all a time," he said. His face was rumpled, crinkled from too many extremes of expression over too many years.

"Jesus God, Sovel." Luke glanced at Marvin, who still slept with his head so oddly tilted. Like the Eager Retard. "Look, you can stay, all right? But just a little while this time. Understand? Sovel?" He couldn't get Sovel's attention. "Sovel? You understand?" He waited.

"Course, Hoop. Fire feels good, don't it?"

3

Knud.

Knud wore loose-fitting shirts with big lopsided collars flapping up and down on his chest as he hurried from one end of the bar to the other.

Waiting on the customers, he had the habit of scratching his forearms and then putting his hands around both empty and half-empty glasses. "Uh-huh?" he grunted; it was his way of saying the conversation bored him, he's heard it before, did you want to drink or what? Sometimes his older sister, Edna—she must have been nearly seventy—tended bar with him. They had a nice way of joking with each other. He was always offering the regulars her telephone number, and she was always threatening to answer if they called.

After we drank the tequila, it was about three-fifteen in the afternoon and time to leave for work.

"Strong stuff," said Matthew, handing Edna the empty bottle. We must have grinned stupidly or crossed our eyes or both.

Edna said sadly, "Look at you."

"On our way," I said. We walked through the driving gray snow to the hot-strip warehouse, a few blocks away.

Russo, the day foreman, was tired and in a hurry to end his shift and go home. So he wouldn't notice we were drunk, we sat on a bench when he gave us instructions. He knew though. He said, "I didn't want you two for this job. You know that? Homo tell you that? Tell him 'Fuck you' for me, would you? I got you down for twelve hours, so I'll see you tomorrow before you leave. Tell him. Okay?"

We picked up a five-gallon thermos, jackhammers, hammer bits, and extra pneumatic hose. We put these and wooden-soled shoes and asbestos suits and gloves in a wheelbarrow. On a rolling flat we piled the pipe frames for nine stories of scaffolding.

Homer checked over our equipment. He muttered something about it not being his usual shift, not his crew. He was more serious than normal. "Looks like a bitch of a job," he shouted above the screech of the overhead cranes and the scream of the gigantic roll-press cylinders through which the slabs were crushed into sheets. He gave us each a small plastic bag of salt tablets. "They'll make you sick if you take too many too fast. Pace yourself up to the top. Pace yourself down." He took us into the foreman's shack, where it was quieter, and gave us gas masks and rope. He explained that as far as he knew the job was to break the firebrick lining out of the smokestack so new lining could be put in the next time that oven went down for repairs. They could only give us the twelve hours time, he said, because time was money and every hour the ovens were turned off figured out to so many thousand dollars of profit lost. "They won't full-fire them until you let them know you're out," he said, "but they're going to be pissed if you hold them back more than twelve hours. If you run late you're supposed to go to the top, lower your equipment down the outside, then come down yourselves on the outside ladder. With this snow, it'll be icy, so go slow."

Matthew stood up on the four-inch wooden soles he had just attached to his work shoes. "They're clumsy," he said.

"*You*'re clumsy," said Homer. "Let me get somebody else for this."

Matthew ignored him. "Double time, right?"

"Asshole," said Homer. He liked Matthew and was no good at hiding it. "Okay. Look, though. Just leave the scaffolding in the stack. I'll have Russo's people take that out on some other shift." He gave us both safety glasses. "Mike," he said to me, but I guess he couldn't remember what he wanted to say. He walked out of the shack.

How can a guy shut a door behind him so the door seems to ask, "Think I ain't got better things to do than bother with you guys?" That, anyway, is how Homer shut the door.

We helped each other with our asbestos suits. Helmets strapped to our heads, safety glasses and black asbestos gloves on, gas masks hanging around our necks, we looked like spacemen. I took big steps as I pulled the cart piled with scaffolding, floated my free hand out in front of me and shouted, "Weightless!" Matthew pushed the wheelbarrow before him toward the entrance to the furnace and looked nervously at the equipment. I pointed to the smokestack rising out of furnace three and disappearing through the warehouse ceiling. "Piece a cake!" I said, but a braking overhead crane made it impossible for even me to hear the words. Then I said it again, quietly and secretly to myself: "Piece a cake."

At the entrance, I pulled Matthew down to a crouch and warned him about the furnace heat and gases. A spark struck off the floor of the furnace could produce a tongue of flame. He knew that, he said. "Take your time," I said, "that's all. Just take your time."

We slowly carried the equipment through the furnace to the throat of the smokestack.

"It's quieter," shouted Matthew at the center where the heat was more intense. My laughter echoed in the furnace a moment and then rushed up the smokestack with the echoing word *quieter*.

"Well, look out!" I shouted in my best imitation of The Attempt. He was a friend of ours. Maybe.

A few days earlier we had been playing b-ball at St. Liz. And it was that kind of sunless afternoon cold where the wind kept troweling a new layer of ice over the pavement we'd shoveled and scraped clean. And then The Attempt wheeled his chair up to us and asked if he could play. He'd given himself another burr haircut. He had on his fatigue-type jacket that said "Tet" in spray-can black on the back. He was wearing his usual crud-covered sunglasses, the ones you could barely see his eyes through. And those eyes—they always looked up toward the hoop. There was something wrong with them, like they couldn't come down or move left or right. I had no idea if he'd ever seen me because I didn't know that I'd ever stood in the path of his sight.

We didn't want him to shoot the hoops with us. He gave

us the creeps. "But, hey, what the hell," Matthew always said after he left. So, he put the ball in The Attempt's hands. "Shoot," he said.

"Look out!" said The Attempt. It was all he ever said. When we talked with him we said things that worked with "Look out!"

I might ask Matthew about his girlfriend. I might say, "How's Irene?"

Matthew would say, "Still seventeen."

The Attempt would say, "Look out!"

We all three would laugh. The Attempt slobbered a little when he laughed, but he had a sense of humor about it.

The Attempt—we didn't know his name because before he got laid off he had worked in the blast furnace and we were in the hot strip—was an "unemployment suicide," the kind you read about in the paper.

The year he tried it was the same year we had two Volks- wagens (within two blocks of each other) go up in flames in our neighborhood. Matthew and I were there when Mr. Beetie came to Mrs. Crismenska's unplanned Rabbit bonfire. "Just like mine," he kept saying, "just like mine. First a little black spot on the hood—then—you can't believe it— flames—everywhere!"

"I ran for my life!" said Mrs. Crismenska.

Mr. Beetie's brother, who was a mechanic and had worked for Caterpillar once, said it was the new VW car- buretors. They just exploded. They were made so they exploded. "Sooner or later," he said, "they'll do that."

The Attempt hung around our neighborhood a lot. I think he grew on us. Either he grew on us or we were just harder up for pals than we thought. The guys who went to college didn't usually come back to Meltenville. That year there was already less production, more and more work given to everybody who wasn't laid off.

It was coming to a stop. It'll still take years before the whole eleven hundred acres of steelworks grinds completely down. But it was coming then and it's still coming.

In our neighborhood, close to the steel mill, you heard people complain sometimes about the lack of pollution. People bitched that the snow got whiter every year. But it was good for The Attempt, I guess. He was more welcome because he was something—even something that made you nervous—which was always going to be there.

That was early November, I think. We finished the last game of HORSE because it'd started snowing again. We said goodbye to The Attempt. He waved his tread-callused right hand at us. He said, "Look out!" I said, "Look out!" Matthew said, "Yeah, look out."

We were renting the bottom half of a big old house; we kept our beer in a little backyard shack, which made a perfect freezer in winter. I got us the last six-packs and brought them into the kitchen. Then, when we'd had a few, we got to talking about God. It's too long to tell about.

Later, I was on my way out for more beer. It was probably nine p.m. We had to leave for work at eleven. I wasn't walking or seeing too good, and Matthew told me I ought to forget the beer. He was joking, of course. I said I'd pray about it. "Hail, Budweiser, full of grace," I said, or something like that. There was a knock on the door.

"Oh, God, that must be God," Matthew said.

It was The Attempt. He waved his hand at us as though he'd been parked outside our door, waving it for the last five or six hours. His bare head was dripping with icy water and his lap was piled with snow. His sunglasses had steamed up and frosted over a little. "Shit!" I said. I should have guessed he wore those sunglasses even at night. "Get in here," Matthew said to him.

"Look out!" said The Attempt and wheeled in.

Matthew got him a dry flannel shirt and some work pants. I was thinking how strange it was going to be, seeing him put those pants on over those dead legs. "I'll make you something hot," I said. "The heat vent's over here." I pointed. I moved a chair so he could park himself near it. He took his sunglasses off to wipe them on the flannel shirt. He looked at me, nodded thanks. His froggy eyes looked at the ceiling light so long I started wondering if he wasn't nearly blind from looking up at the sun and ceiling lights all the time.

Matthew was always ahead of me. "Did you get lost in the snow?" he asked.

The Attempt put his sunglasses back on. He brushed the snow off his lap and into the flannel shirt. He pivoted the chair and took the snow-filled shirt to the front door where he shook it out. He gave it and the pants back to Matthew.

"Well, stay here for the night, anyway," Matthew said. "You can sleep in Michael's bed."

I told him yeah, he was welcome to it and, as a matter of fact, that was awfully nice of Matthew to offer my bed. "Only be careful about the bedbugs," I said. "They're piranha-size."

The Attempt looked over in my direction like he was looking at a tree on the side of a hill miles away. I think he wanted to smile. I said, "No kidding. The bugs'll chew on you all night. You can wake up with half of you gone."

I didn't realize what I'd said until I watched him lift himself from his chair to the bed and drag his thin legs like two lengths of chain after him.

Later, on the walk to the hot strip I told Matthew about it and how it made me think of other things. I asked, "You ever think about Luke? Like about what he might be doing some night there in Enchantmentland?"

He was quiet. Usually we tried to be numb-drunk when we went to work, but we weren't that time. And it was a long night.

"Bet T.A.'s left," I said on our walk home in the morning.

"No," Matthew said. He took long, risky strides over the iced sidewalks.

"Probably sick as a dog," I said.

"No."

At the back door to the house I asked, "You think knocking might scare him?"

Matthew knocked on the door. We heard The Attempt saying, "Look out. Look out." He was saying it the way you'd say, "I'm coming. I'm coming," so I didn't get my keys out.

Matthew was plenty tired and maybe not feeling too good. He went directly to sleep. I offered The Attempt some orange juice but he wasn't interested. "You've dried out," I said.

His sunglasses lifted a little on the bridge of his nose. It wasn't a smile. I told him he was welcome to stay. I told him we'd be getting up for basketball about noon and he could come if he wanted. Half an hour later I fell asleep wondering what had got into me.

In our game of HORSE later, we got to talking about a lot of things. Matthew said we had to buy a car so we could drive to New Mexico and see Luke. We talked about the foreign cars, about how good Datsuns and Toyotas were but so flimsy you could die if you hit a speed bump too fast; about how American small cars were designed to kill themselves if they didn't kill you.

"Look out!" said The Attempt.

"He got an 'E' yet?" I asked.

Matthew said, "You got an 'E'?"

The Attempt passed the ball to me.

"Well," I said, "let's make it HORSEBUTT and you can stay in."

"When we get a car, we want a big back seat, anyway," Matthew said.

I sank my famous center-court hook shot. Matthew missed it, so he had a 'B.' The Attempt wheeled and dribbled out to center court. His sunglasses were pointed ten feet over the backboard but his neck and shoulders were poised like the way geese do alighting on water. He sank the shot.

"Damn!" I said. When he got hot on court The Attempt didn't miss a shot. It was a matter of record. He made a left-handed set shot from the key. Matthew and I were both righties. We barely hit the rim.

"Look out!" said The Attempt. Pretty soon Matthew got his last 'T.' I had a 'U' and not a prayer of winning.

"I think I ought to look at colleges," said Matthew.

"What?" I couldn't believe him. He would bring it up now and then, but our plans for the sign painting business always won.

"Right. Colleges," I said. I missed my shot. "Hands're cold."

Matthew said, "You've got a 'T,' Michael."

"I know it, okay?"

"What have you got?" he said to The Attempt, who'd wheeled in a beaut of an underhand lay-up.

I said, "I think he's got a 'B.'"

It didn't matter. The ball came off my palm instead of my fingertips and my shot missed.

"Well, look out!" said Matthew. "We're horsebutts again."

He had a good sense of humor. And I always liked it, except I had figured out something: it was always just a tick or tock ahead of mine.

On the walk home we bought some more beer; I shoved my freezing hands deep in my jacket pockets and Matthew didn't make me carry it. The Attempt had the basketball in his lap. His sunglasses were steamed over and even a little frosted. He was wheeling himself just ahead of us, his bare hands on that icy rubber.

Matthew and I didn't even nod at each other until the second beer back at the apartment. The Attempt was cooking us some toasted cheese sandwiches. He went right to our icebox and started putting it all on the counter.

"Have we got a live-in cook?" I asked. I don't know why I was so worried The Attempt would stay.

The phone rang and, naturally, it was Irene. Matthew and she made some arrangements. He said he'd be back in time for work.

"Fuck," I said. I was going to add, "if you get the chance, " but I was too slow.

"Okay. I'll try." He said it just that quick.

Later, I drank his beer and mine both. The Attempt had one too. At about three I asked if he wanted to try making the three-thirty showing at the Columbus Theater. He didn't shrug yes or no or even say his only two words.

We got there a few minutes late. We sat in the back so he'd have a place to park himself. The movie was one of those space thrillers with aliens and humans teamed against machines. Everything is metal in those movies. The spaceships are gleaming metal arrowheads. All the death weapons and death traps are steely and perfect and work in ways steel things don't work and never will.

So, I was getting kind of disgusted with the whole thing when The Attempt started rocking in his chair and whispering his warning.

"Hey," I said.

You could just barely hear him above the grinding and screaming noises of the steely movie. He didn't stop. He rocked left and right. He rocked up and down. He whispered.

"Hey. Stop it. And take your sunglasses off, stupid."

He moved a row back. The girl he had set his wheelchair next to put her little hand around his and said, "Hush, T.A.," and he shut up completely. It didn't surprise me that she recognized him because almost everybody in town had seen or at least heard of The Attempt. (He went to everywhere and back in his wheelchair.) What got me was him shutting up like that. I had thought his mind was a match for his two words, blown as his two blown eyes and legs. But here this twelve or thirteen-year-old girl said, "Hush," and woke him up out of what was only a bad dream.

An hour later he started in again. He whispered it. He reached his arm down and he poked me. "Look out," he said.

I turned around. "Jesus, T.A., would you—can't you control it?" That didn't work at all. I tried the girl's trick. "Hush, goddamit," I said.

He rocked his chair. He hollered, "Look out! Look out!" The girl put her hands around his. The usher came; he said, "Take him out of here," to the girl. She looked at me. He pointed the light at my chest and then my face. "You—take him out." Together, the usher and I pushed his wheelchair out of the Columbus. "Look out!" T.A. screamed hoarsely, "Look out!"

I thought the little girl would come out with us, but she didn't. How did I know it wasn't all a dream he was having? His shoulders didn't move. His head didn't move. "Look out! Look out! Look out!"

When we got back to the apartment he was more hoarse. He wheeled himself real slow to the door.

"You finished?" I asked. "If you're finished you're welcome in."

He shifted himself in his chair. He wiped the ice slush from his wheels and came inside with me.

Later, I got to thinking I'd treated him too much like a bad dog or something. I made us some soup and hot chocolate and asked him what section of the paper he wanted. I gave him the whole thing. He put it in his lap and turned the pages like his eyes could really read. We both felt better.

That night on the walk to the hot strip, Matthew asked me how it went.

"We saw a movie," I said. "You?"

He didn't say anything. I thought that must mean he and Irene spent the afternoon in bed. Matthew was that kind of a guy who joked about it sometimes but kept it his business. I figured that was fair to Irene, who probably didn't want to be talked about, and I admired that in him.

An hour into the shift, Matthew said, "We broke up." He kept on sweeping the floor of the weighing shack we were in.

"Damn, Matthew. Damn," I said. His face was unchanged. "Did you see it coming?"

"Since it started."

"Yeah?" I thought about that real hard. "Yeah?"

"Yeah."

"Well. Damn." I was stupid to feel anything for him. He wasn't feeling anything. "How come?" I said. He took off his safety hat, pushed his hair into order and put the hat back on.

"Forget it," he said.

We left the shack and walked back out into the noise of the warehouse, where the sheet steel coils cooled under the weak light of giant, stooped lamps. The stubborn dumbness of our life in Meltenville lit up in me and smoldered for a couple of hours.

At the end of our three a.m. lunchbreak I couldn't help myself. "Was it the college talk? Was that what ruined things?"

He gave me a famous Matthew looney look. We picked up our brooms and stood.

"I'm not making a case against her or something," he said.

"I know that, but—"

"But shut the fuck up, huh?" She's seventeen years old, for Christ's sake! I'm almost twenty and maybe I'm going to do something—clean the ash off me, maybe, so I won't be taken for some—you know."

I thought I knew: some steelmill broom-pusher.

At five or so we took a coffee break. I wanted to talk just friendly talk. I said, "You remember shucking corn for Lofters a few years ago? You remember that gluey stuff that collects on your hands?"

"Huh?"

"Your hands get all gluey when you shuck corn."

"Right," he said. He said it like "So?"

When my conversation is chopped off, it branches out. "Well, I just never liked that stickiness, Matthew. You couldn't wash it all off, I remember. 'There's a lesson here,' Mr. Lofter said one time when I asked him how to get the stuff off. There *was* a lesson there: every time you asked Mr. Lofter any question, he'd always say, 'There's a lesson here.' And then never give you any idea what it might be. You ever notice that?"

He said, "Michael." Then he interrupted himself and said, "Mae Buskovitcz let me put my hands up her shirt."

"When?"

"On Lofter's farm. In the middle of his field."

I laughed. "Is she the one you called Maybe?"

"She's the one." He relaxed his arms. He set his coffee on his knee. "So I grabbed hold of them and told her I was stuck. That I couldn't get my hands off. That we'd have to go in to Lofter's house and soap up her chest and my hands. She played right along."

"That's great, that's brilliant!"

"It was, you know it?" He looked at me real long, like he wanted to see if I appreciated how really brilliant he was. It hurt me that he had to check me out that way. He looked hard in my eyes, like did I recognize him?

I got gradually mad all over again. It just came up in me. "Matthew," I asked, "why's it so much easier to work with you when we're both drunk?"

He slowly shook his head, giving himself a quiet order not to say something smartassed.

We didn't talk then, except for him saying in the mill showers, "Day off."

At the apartment, The Attempt was asleep in his wheelchair. His head was thrown back and his blue-black hair stood up like a just-struck match. The way his lips were, he might have been calling someone by name.

We tried not to wake him up. We started coffee and got into our sweatclothes. Taking the coffee mugs and b-ball out with us, we picked up the shovel and the broom and went to work on a section of court at St. Liz. Finally we could play, but it was so windy lots of times we almost missed the rim. We agreed to play one game of PIG. Enough to get the game out of our systems and quit. Then T.A. showed up.

Matthew said hi and told him, "Michael's got an 'I' and is about ready to lose. Want in on the next game?"

He did. We played HORSE and then HORSEBUTT and lost to him, and Matthew said, "We're horsebutts again," and The Attempt said, "Look out!" We carried the shovel and broom and basketball back to the apartment. Matthew checked the mailbox. "I wish he'd write us more," he said.

"Luke's a busy man," I said, which made us both laugh.

Sooty snow was drifted up against the door, and sooty snow was piled on the roof. "They must've fired furnaces one and two," I said.

"Ten in the morning." Matthew kicked the snow on the porch. He lifted his head up to look at me.

"The damn ash isn't my fault," I said. He didn't look away from me.

Inside, The Attempt lifted himself from his wheelchair onto the floor. "Look out," he said as a way of asking for permission to sleep.

"Sure," I said. I left to get some beer. I bought Matthew a peace-offering six-pack. But when I got home he was asleep too.

They slept until a little after five; I made us all some canned soup when they woke up. "Beer in the icebox," I said. I hadn't bought enough.

By six o'clock it was pitch dark out and the snow had gotten worse. The Attempt sat in his wheelchair and looked out the window.

Matthew said he was going out, but he changed his mind and sat down in the lounger across from where I sat at the kitchen table. We watched television. It was half an hour before I realized the program was the same sci-fi movie T.A. and I had just a day ago paid seven bucks to see. "They've got this on at the Columbus," I said. "It's the same damn—"

"I'm not going anywhere," Matthew said, his eyes fixed

on the TV. "I mean college or anything like that. I didn't mean to piss you off, you know."

Instantly. That's the way he did things sometimes: instant as a pass and tip in. "Don't worry, okay?" I said. "Say one Our Father, a dozen Hail Marys, take two rosaries, call me in the morning."

"It's not funny, Michael. I just wanted you to know."

"I'm sorry, too," I said, wanting my not-very-clever cleverness back.

The Attempt wheeled his chair around and faced it toward Matthew.

"You been listening?" I asked.

"Of course he has," said Matthew. "Hey, T.A.," he said, "should I ever leave?"

"Look out."

"Should I stay?"

"Look out."

"Should we do the sign business, me and Michael? Should we buy a car? Should we go to Enchantmentland?"

Then The Attempt did something he'd done once before. He quickly pushed himself across the room. He pulled the coats from the closet. And he threw them at us.

"Come on," I said. "No."

Matthew said, "No, T.A."

The Attempt shook his head, nearly knocking his sunglasses off. He pushed his chair so close to me that the arms of it met the arms of mine. "Look out," he said.

I asked Michael to give me my coat.

"Look out!" he shouted ahead of us.

The fly ash and the wet air made a kind of coffee-colored fog that closed behind him as he broke his wheelchair through it and weaved us in and out of the neighborhood. Away from our neighborhood but close enough to reach us, we heard cars honking at each other. We could hear the presses in the steelworks groan. The train lines that run through the works were still, but they gasped as if they couldn't stay still much longer.

"Look out!" We followed him past the new apartments in the neighborhood, six months old and so badly built they'd slumped in their foundations and shivered off some of their shiny white siding. Everywhere that we saw parked cars we passed JESUS SAVES and HONK IF YOU ARE JESUS bumper stickers. You Dam Right was lit up, but soundless. I'd never seen it like that before, like a little fire burning pointlessly.

The Attempt wheeled us through the bar's gravel parking lot. A couple of cars were idling and the men and women in them held onto each other. Further on, we could see the big neon Baseball Cardinals sign out on the edge of town. It was lit all year long. "It's A Home Run!!!" the sign said, one flaming blue letter at a time, and then the exclamation points, and then all lit at once, and then dark.

It seemed like every home was lighted up with one of those big spotlights glowing over its front or back yard. Dogs rattled their icy chain leashes.

"Look out!" he said all the way to the house, where the sagging clotheslines criss-crossing the backyard lashed in the wind.

"Look out! Look out! Look out!" Even after we were inside, he was saying it. He muttered it all night long.

Once, I said, "Shut up," and he shut up. For about thirty seconds.

Real late, maybe three or four in the morning, I whispered, "Matthew?" I tried again: "Matthew?"

"I'm here," he said. "I'm not going anywhere."

The Attempt was asleep, finally. I had time to think. I sat up in bed and listened to that good steely snow hit the windows, and I knew there would be more work. It made me feel better. In a way, I had decided things for both of us. But I thought it was okay because we were planning to get out. I was sure we could.

·

The second Friday in December when Luke visited Michael, he brought Marvin and Sovel with him. He knew Michael wouldn't be exactly appreciative, but Sovel tricked him into it. "You ashamed of us?" Sovel had asked. Luke was prepared to answer yes to Sovel but not to Marvin.

Sovel had read perfectly his uncertainty. "Ashamed of poor Marvin, huh?" he said.

Luke didn't know how to answer. At Michael's he introduced them as "a couple buddies over staying at my place." He pronounced it "overstaying."

Sovel announced himself as "a prodigal friend a Luke's" and "a new friend a the family, I hope." He extended a firm handshake to both Michael and Ruth ("Sovel, ma'am"), nodding his head. "Heard lots about you. Can we come in?" He stepped inside. "Close the door, Marvin. This here's Marvin."

"Hello," said Marvin.

Ruth led the two men into the living room of the narrow trailer. At the door, Michael took Luke's box of basket-balls and yardsticks. His face shielded by the box, he said, "They're pretty mangy, Luke." Michael's voice was deliberate; his hands were too steady for him to be sober.

"Sorry, Michael, I couldn't help it."

"The big one—Marvin?—he looks Indian, like Ruth."

"He is."

Michael put the box in a corner behind the door. "She'll be glad."

As Luke walked into the kitchen, Ruth was setting two extra places, and Marvin was asking the baby's name. When Marvin held out his hands to Clair, she leaned forward in her highchair to take one big finger in each fist. "Pretty hair," he said. He blew into her dark bangs and asked Ruth, "You're Tewa?" She nodded.

Sovel said, "Marvin here's an Acoma. Full. I married his sister Telopa, had a no-good, runaway daughter by her and then Telopa died in '58. Acoma women ain't supposed to marry whites. Well, her people said she died of Albuquerque, like Albuquerque was the name of a disease, right? Taken care of Marvin since he took ill in '61."

"Let's eat," said Michael. He took a beer from the refrigerator.

"Wouldn't mind one at-tall," Sovel said, reaching out his hand. "That's twenty years I taken care of him."

When Ruth served the meal, Sovel and Marvin ate with such energy and concentration they reminded Luke of machinery. Michael, who always ate very little, mixed himself a drink and watched them. He mouthed the word *Wow!* to Luke, who asked the two men, "You hungry?"

"Boy," said Sovel in a gasp between bites. Marvin did not look up.

"Good beer," said Sovel, shaking the can to show it was empty. Ruth brought him another. "Him too," Sovel said, nodding at Marvin.

After Ruth had fed Clair and wiped the child's hands and face, she gave her to Luke. She asked Marvin and Sovel if they would like more of the stew. "I'll have to warm up more," she said when she received no answer.

Acting annoyed at being interrupted in his attack on the food, Sovel said, "Right. And more bread." In a me-too gesture, Marvin raised his head and opened his leaden eyes wide.

Clair, sitting on Luke's lap, giggled at Marvin's expression. Marvin did it again for her. "Thanks plenty," he said when Ruth returned with a new plate of bread and butter.

"Her name is Clair," Marvin said, pointing a loaded fork. It was the kind of simple but enthusiastic statement of fact that Luke had discovered was characteristic of him.

Ruth said, "Yes."

"Clair," said the child.

"With an *i*?"

Sovel, not looking up from his plate, said, "Two big brown ones, looks like." He laughed. No one enjoyed Sovel more than Sovel did. "I'll have another a them," he said as Michael opened the refrigerator. "Thanks."

"Well, Clair," said Marvin, "do you sing yet?"

"She's pretty little for—" Michael began.

"Yes," Ruth said. She served more stew and ignored Michael's confused glance.

"Good," Marvin said. Filling his plate again, he picked

up his knife and raised it like a student needing attention. "Where's the john?"

Michael said, "Behind you. Near the front door."

"Excuse me." Marvin placed his fork on the full plate of food and took the plate and a slice of bread with him to the bathroom.

"Jesus." Michael pushed his own plate away.

For the first time, Sovel put his elbows down on the table. "Wish he wouldn't do that," he said. "The man must have a bowel only so long is what I say." He held up his right little finger.

"Damn," Michael said.

"I seen him maybe just a month ago eat a whole meal on the can."

Luke said, "Okay, Sovel."

"Well, it ain't pretty. But what is? What I say is most ugly things make more sense than pretty things anyhow." Luke glared at him.

Sovel rose from his chair. "Great stew," he said to Ruth.

At the bathroom door Sovel knocked. "Marv, you all right?" His stropped voice sounding chipped, even gentle, he asked, "Can you finish up, Marv? You're stirring up these folks juices."

When the two men returned to the table, Marvin's lips were discolored. Large deep-red blotches had formed above and below his left eye. "Sorry," he said weakly as he sat down.

Sovel stood behind him. "Really. He really is."

Marvin looked at Clair as if to ask for her understanding.

"He ain't too good," Sovel said, drawing attention to himself with the confidentiality in his voice.

Ruth brought cups of coffee. Sovel took Marvin's cup, explaining, "He don't drink it. But I don't let it go to waste if I got cream and sugar with it."

Clair took the napkin from Marvin's clenched hand. "Here," she said, giving it back, "yours."

"Clair?" said Marvin; his eyes were almost closed. "Clair?" He mumbled something else. He lowered his shoulders.

"Me," the child said. She said it to everyone, then. "Me."

"Brain problems," Sovel said calmly, "Luke'll tell you— bad case." He tested the coffee. He put in more sugar.

Marvin's head lowered beneath his shoulders. "Clair," he mumbled, his voice thick. The child stepped back from him.

Uncertain whether this was The Routine, Luke was angered. "Sovel?" he said.

"He gets bad and gets all right and bad again and you can't stop him. Is that real cream?" He put some in Marvin's cup and sipped at it. "He'll be okay, Marv. Marv?"

Everyone was caught up by the music of Sovel's voice and the absolute quiet of Marvin.

"Marv?" Sovel swallowed coffee. "Some times are worse than others."

Marvin's eyes were closed now. Twitching like a thing trying to escape, his right arm lay on the table before him. By degrees, he lowered his head more and then his shoulders. He began to bend forward at the waist.

Clair whimpered. She retreated to Luke's lap, but she reached her arms out as if wanting to hold Marvin.

"Hell, he'll be okay. Won't you, Marv?" Sovel slapped Marvin's back.

The thought of Marvin finally resting his head on the uncontrolled arm frightened Luke. "Sovel!"

"What do we do?" Michael asked. His face was beaded with sweat.

Sovel looked at him. "Luke'll tell you: can't do a damn thing. Happens almost ever meal."

"Like hell!" said Luke.

"Right," said Sovel without flinching. "Like clockwork. Like he's got some alarm set in him can't be changed and can't be turned off."

Michael pleaded with Sovel, "Can't we do something?"

Luke stood. "Marvin," he said, "cut it out."

"I've got him to a doctor once or twiced," said Sovel, "but they just give him a subscription."

"God," Michael said.

Marvin's forehead pressed into his arm; low on the back of his head, almost at the tip of his spine, part of the tumor was visible. Both Marvin's arm and body convulsed.

"Marvin," Luke said. "Sovel."

Sovel said, "In Albuquerque a—"

Clair, her arms still outstretched, struggled to get free of Luke and reach Marvin. Her scream grew more pitched.

"Like I say," said Sovel above her cries, "in Albuquerque a doctor give us a subscription for some pills just stopped it cold."

Ruth took Clair and carried her, her arms flailing, outside.

Sovel was in control. "Pills were expensive as a woman a means. Worked though."

Neither Luke nor Michael could even turn to look at each other. Now, Marvin huffed and heaved. Everything about him, even his smell, was buffalo-like—his great bowed shoulders, his angular jaw and chin, his eyes set high on his face, the coarse black hair on the back of his neck, all of him. And one more thing Luke noticed as if seeing it through Michael: the few hairs on Marvin's chin and neck were dark, stiff, like the apron of hair on a buffalo's chin. It was the kind of beard he had seen in the last pictures of his brother Matthew.

"Even a little relief is a thankful lot is what I say," said Sovel. "If I had the money—"

Michael had already taken his wallet out. He flung dollar bills at Sovel and at Luke. "Get them out, Luke. When I come back, have them out of here!" His face was streaming with tears as he walked out of the trailer. He called for Ruth and Clair.

It was late before Marvin was able to move. Sovel and Luke supported him through the wind together but did not speak to each other.

Finally, kicking the light covering of snow to get Luke's attention, Sovel said, "Heavy Indian, huh?" Near Romelia's bee boxes, Luke shifted more of Marvin's weight onto his right shoulder.

Sovel said, "See her?"

"What?" Luke said. "Who?" Like a mist, the slender Chicana had hovered at the base of his thoughts for the entire walk. Now she rose in to him all at once, taking every branch and bud in her cool, enlivening grip.

"We're closer," said Sovel.

"I—her?"

Sovel raised his head from its place near Marvin's chest. "Good," he pointed to the hut. "There she is."

4

Pulling our gas masks over our faces, we began building the first floor of scaffolding to bring us into the stack. The heat and the vapor from the slab-oven floor made the dust on our glasses shimmer and even our own arms and hands kind of wavered before us. The thick wooden soles buckled onto our work shoes were awkward, and we could have taken them off after walking through the oven, but we forgot. When we tried fitting a pipe section diagonally into our scaffolding, my section hit the floor. Afraid of the smoking sparks that burst into the air, we both jumped back with that slow, exaggerated movement you make in deep water. We bumped into each other. Through our masks the laughter sounded like it wasn't ours, like a third person stood somewhere near who laughed for us. Matthew tugged his mask down and shouted, "Edna's tequila!"

I shouted back that we'd make the base of the scaffolding in her honor. Pulling his mask on again, he tilted his head back and looked directly up the throat of the smokestack. "To Edna." He said it weakly. We fit the two five-by-eight pieces of wooden flooring onto the scaffold, Matthew handing the equipment up to me.

"It's quieter," he said, his voice rattling hollowly through the mask and echoing. It nearly scared me how much quieter it was at this level, which was probably a circumference of twenty feet. From only one story up, the screech of the cranes and scream of the machinery was a single vague cry already sounding a great distance below us. I connected the hammer bit to my jackhammer and arranged its long coiled pink hose safely behind me. Matthew imitated me, and we both hoisted the hammers to our waists, pushing the bits downward into the brick. In the deep quiet of the smokestack the machine-gun noise was insignificant.

It took us almost an hour to bring down the first six-foot-wide band of faint red brick and another half an hour to pickax the stubborn pieces. Then we broomed the crud from our boards and recoiled the tangled hoses. Matthew set his jackhammer down and pulled his glasses off to rub the lenses clean. The clownface of dust fringing his cheeks and forehead made his deep-set eyes look startled. "Long way," he said, looking up the shaft above us.

"Like the neck of a Budweiser bottle, Matthew."

He reached for the large thermos in one corner of our scaffold. "Best to wait," I said. "Sit a while." We sat on the two piles of coiled hose and looked at our work. "Good job."

He didn't hear me. "Wouldn't you," he said, "like to make one of those big Budweiser signs? Trace out that mean eagle on the label?"

"A house-size bottle," I said, "with sexy drops of sweat rolling off it." It was one of our favorite things to do, talking about making The Big Sign. Matthew usually liked to talk about actually making it, while I liked to pretend I was some driver seeing it, awestruck by it. "There's a sign that says, 'Cold!' " I said.

"And if you have the Clydesdales on it, it says, 'Powerful.' Or 'Pure.' "

Our words hissed at a slow, strange rate through the masks. We might as well have been speaking another language.

As the idea of the Clydesdales took hold in him, Matthew spoke more excitedly. "Imagine marching those beauties across the sky like that. Every hoof and wither and haunch a little different."

"Which ones strain the hardest?" I asked. "The ones closest or furthest from the wagon?"

"Furthest," he said like he knew, like we were right there standing on some scaffolding in front of a one-hundred-square-yard sign, lifting finished paper Clydesdales into the sky and sticking them there for good.

It was great to talk about, to imagine the snowy hills the Clydesdales galloped over, the stream in the foreground where their powerful legs were reflected, the "team" (Michael's idea) of massive snowclouds overhead—we went on and on.

"Then, before we finish," I said, "we put a big, steaming pile of horseshit in one of the lower corners and paint our fluorescent 'M&M Signs' mark on it."

"Or—or," he said, his head fixed on the vision of it, "eagle shit that could be just a real spot on one of the Clydesdales or could be—maybe just the two of us could tell—eagle shit."

I said, "There's a sign that says, 'Truthful!' "

Without having to signal each other, we got up and built the next level of scaffolding. It was about seven p.m. We had already been working for three hours of our twelve-hour shift.

.

In the hut, Luke and Sovel laid Marvin down and covered him with the greatcoat Sovel had worn on the day a week earlier when he and Marvin arrived. Marvin's teeth rattled. His chin bore further into his chest. Luke rearranged the coat to protect more of the giant-shouldered man against the cold.

"Is this a dishwasher coat?" he asked Marvin, who remained quiet.

Sovel said, "It's stole. I took it out a fancy car in a parking lot few months ago in Albuquerque."

"Christ," said Luke.

"Don't Christ *or* Jesus me, Luke. I coulda took the car—had keys in it and groceries in the back seat."

"What got into you?" Luke asked.

"Marvin. Marvin said no. Probably had a full tank a gas. Probably—"

"You listened to Marvin. Since when?"

"That's plain unkind of you, Luke. He said between us we'd buy one with dishwashing money. It'd be fun, he said." Sovel looked down at Marvin. "I knew it then he was sick for good. Knew it and worked the job for another two months anyway.

"Car was a '57 Chrysler Imperial, had a heater size of a small oven. So. We left it be. Froze our asses off in an alley lean-to, fried our hands off shoving plates in racks—for 'fun.'" He scowled at Marvin. He ran his hands over the greatcoat. "Good cloth," he said, his broken upper teeth appearing behind an admiring grin.

"You tired as me?" Sovel asked.

"I don't have a car you can take," Luke said.

Sovel lay down close to Marvin. "Plain unkind, Luke."

It was very still in the hut then. Luke was thankful there was no wind; the chill was enough. He positioned himself on his side in the darkest corner.

"Luke, you still go with Katy outa the Gospel Rescue?"

"That's none of your business, you know."

"I know." Sovel chuckled. "Heh?"

"No. I see her now and then, though."

"Hope spurts eternal," Sovel said.

"Yeah."

"You gone to the Fortham Parlor lately?"

"The funeral home?"

Sovel made a slurping noise. "With the big banquets for the wakes."

"You're a ghoul," Luke said.

"I get hungry enough I'm a lot a things."

"You're right on that count."

"Everybody is."

Luke heard Sovel say something more but—he was thankful—could not distinguish the words.

Turning on his other side, Luke looked out the hut window-hole at the bottlebrush and other scrub animated by the moonlight on the gleaming mesa, a black wave frozen at its crest.

He fell asleep hearing Sovel's mumbled fast-talk. Sovel seemed to be giving himself some kind of instructions. But Luke was swept by the image of the black wave out to the jumbled ocean of his dreams.

All the black viscera of the steel mill—the blast furnaces, the coke ovens, the hot strip rolling mill and the smokestacks rising over it, the overhead cranes and slag-laden trains— bellowed and expanded and bellowed again, crowding each other, joining, melting into a smoking blue-white sea and then a single great pure wave of red molten ore. "Michael!" he said. "Matthew!" He backed away from it in steps that carried him a tremendous distance. Before him, his brothers held their places, their hands locked together like small children. They danced before the horrible wave; when the shadow of its crest fell over them they laughed and danced more wildly. He backed away, further west. The heat made them blue-white, it changed them into dancing, transparent-glass objects. When they turned a final time to wave at Luke, he saw a very tiny reflection of himself in their hardening glass faces. He was very far away from them.

They spun around and dove into the center of the wave as it fell.

"Perfect." The dull edge of Sovel's voice woke Luke up.

His eyes still shut, he heard Sovel repeating, "Okay, Marv. Marv?" Marvin's animal moan filled the small hut. "Shhh," said Sovel, "you'll wake him up." He asked, "Luke? You awake?"

Luke's eyes were narrowly opened, but he was sure his position hid them. He watched as Sovel leaned over the huge figure in the dark. "Luke?" Sovel asked again. "Listen, Marv, you gotta—you better—understand?" His voice was like metal scraped against glass. "You better get you together."

He rearranged the coat over Marvin and brushed and dusted it with his hand. "Good coat's a perfect hide is what I always say."

Marvin's breathless whimpers were muffled in the coat collar Sovel pulled over his chin and cheek. "Get it the hell out and over with," said Sovel, sounding more frustrated than angry. "I'm sleeping some now and I don't want to hear that sniveling." Sovel again lay next to Marvin. He grunted a good-night. Luke thought he saw him put his hands behind his head or over his ears. The longer Luke looked into the darkness the more clearly he saw Sovel's bony elbows pointing skyward like hooks. He began to consider what Sovel had said about getting it over with but was too weary to think about it longer. He closed his eyes.

Marvin's uneven breathing, whistled through clenched teeth, returned Luke to the glittering blizzard. He and Michael were huddled together, waiting, waiting for Matthew to emerge from the red wave. The sound of the wave was dreadful—a fusing of the roiling flames with the fading voice of water reverberating inside.

Luke woke up with the feel of Michael's frozen grip on his shoulders and a vision of his brother's brittle body leaning against him, his eyes transparent.

Sovel was also awake again. The moonlight now reached through the hut window hole and illuminated the sitting figure. He was a curious fat man; like hard, tight-skinned balloons, his face bulged and shone, his big rigid stomach floated before his small hips.

His whispering clarified with emotion, Sovel patted the creature he sat next to. "Hell, Marv. It's real bad—all day bad, huh?" He lowered his head closer to Marvin's. "I didn't know." He ran his sleeve over his eyes. "I wouldna been mean if I knew how bad." Sovel lay his head on the dirt at Marvin's side and he tried to meet his eyes. He pushed his stubby fingers through Marvin's hair and lightly over the tumor at the base of his skull. "Marv? Marv, I never know how to know no more." Sovel shifted to his knees.

Then a thing happened that Luke had thought impossible: Sovel pressed his face into the depression between Marvin's shoulder blades and wept. He did not lift his head. He did not once shift his weight.

An hour later, at sunrise, Sovel shook Luke. "Luke," he asked, "can I build him a fire?" Luke nodded. "You slept hard last night, huh?" said Sovel.

"Did I?"

Sovel left the hut.

Marvin was quiet but awake still, his head twisted awry, his open eyes inert. "You okay?" Luke asked. The spot low on the back of Marvin's head, almost at the top of his spine, was more swollen than Luke had noticed at first. "My God. How long has it been this bad?" Bending to be closer to Marvin, Luke said, "Can you hear when you're—like this?"

"Soful," Marvin grunted.

"He's gone for scrap. He's planning on making you a fire." He thought he saw Marvin smile. "Maybe Sovel's changed a little, huh?" Luke considered that for a moment. "It makes me nervous."

Sovel returned. He pushed the wood into the dug-out corner of the hut where Luke built fires, and he flooded it with kerosene and lit it. It whooshed to a start. "There," said Sovel, "a fire. And better'n an extra blanket is what I always say." When the fire threatened to burn low, Sovel fanned it. When it collapsed, he added more scrap wood to keep it going until the sun finally lit the broken-slatted roof of the hut. As he gathered the embers into a pile, he said, "We're gonna see to you, Marv. Me and Luke."

The Walgreen's in the new mall in Las Almas opened at nine o'clock. It was a long walk to that particular drugstore but Sovel had insisted. The medicine they spent Michael's money on was an over-the-counter box of sleeping pills, a prescription bottle of pain-killer, and a half pint of scotch for Sovel.

"Hello, Mr. Hoop," said the checker, the same handsome Chicana he had seen at Bogel's. She was working with another clerk, and the line at the counter moved slowly. "I'll ring this one," she told the young clerk. Her wrists moved with the same resolute strength he had noticed in her narrow waist and straight back.

She took the money from Sovel, pushed his five dollar bill into its place in the register drawer and pulled a twenty out. "But, ma'am, he—" said the clerk as she handed the bill to Sovel. She placed the things in the bag and put it in Luke's hands. "For the trick. With the basketball," she said. "And you," she said to the clerk, "pay attention."

When they stepped outside, Luke asked, "You know her?"

"Met her here day we come in," said Sovel.

"Did she give you money then, too?"

"Nice lady, huh?"

It was pointless to ask more; nevertheless, Luke handed Sovel the bottle of scotch and asked if he knew her name.

"How the hell do I know the name of every bitch with a weakness for hobos?" Sovel opened the bottle. "New stores sure smell nice, don't they?" He swallowed. "You go on and I'll meet you at your place. I got business in town."

The sun was bright and direct but no match for the sharp wind that blew from south to north across Luke's face on the walk back. In a small enclosed field behind Fred Huff's farm a bonfire of tree limbs burned. The smoke formed golden-black shoulders that would start to rise and straighten, only to be humbled by the wind into chalky fingers disintegrating just as they gripped the earth.

When Luke had first come to Las Almas he had walked these chile and cotton farms; the first afternoon, he had gotten on all fours in the center of one of the fields, felt the winter earth on his palms and knees and on the tops of his feet, felt the sun full on his back. It was the first he understood of how the gritty wind, the sun—as well as every shunted snakeskin, leaf corpse, cactus needle, coyote jaw, tumbleweed, devil's claw—all hone the desert and the earth of the Rio Grande valley. Rounded stones become dull blades, broken clods of earth break into shards. A man could hold himself to the earth here and feel the husk cutting away from the seed.

Now, so much time gone, Luke understood better how it was that he had become a hobo. No man was meant to be shut up in a smothering warehouse, trying to have all the qualities of the steel itself, asking himself, "What am I making?"

His dad had wanted to make more than the steel of corrugated roofs and bridge forms, garages and barns, warehouses and stadiums high as Babel.

Luke remembered a particular afternoon in which his dad had come out to shoot the basketball with him and Michael and Matthew. Matthew was about seven years old; Michael, ten.

"Damn," said Michael when he saw him walk down the back porch steps, "lookit."

"Pass me the ball, boys." He was not drunk, but not completely sober. He held the ball high above and just before him, and made his whole body, head to toe, a deadweight pedestal for the spring of his arms. The tips of his fingers were cocked more assuredly than his head. He did not shoot. "It would have been my dad's birthday today," he said.

"Great," said Michael, wincing.

"I tell you—I tell you what, my dad was what you'd call a serious man." He lowered the basketball to his waist. "His favorite thing he said was, 'Shoot or shut up.' And he made me play basketball like a figure skater. Every move was supposed to be *a move*."

Matthew looked at Luke to avoid looking anywhere else. "So?" said Luke.

He raised the ball up, steadied himself, shot. The ball shivered on the front of the rim and tipped itself out. "I need to tighten that rim," he said. "I tell you what," he said to Matthew because he knew he could always make Matthew listen when his other sons wouldn't. "Do you know how my Dad died? You know? I'll tell you.

"Soup." He wiped his nose with the back of his thumb. He

was wearing only a T-shirt and light slacks, and the air was late-February Illinois air. "My Dad. Worked his ass off in the mill. Didn't—never made—made enough.

"So. My mother made soup. Almost every night. Soup. He cussed, begged, he threatened her—gave in every meal. It left him hungry was what he said. It made him ashamed, you know it.

"She never believed in him. Banked up his money so when he died we'd be safe, her and me."

Luke put his arms out at his waist. "Okay," his dad said, and snapped the ball hard at him. "Hell with it, then." He started to walk back into the house. Coming back, he crouched before Matthew.

"Matthew. Don't be that way. It was just a joke." He took Matthew's waist into his large hands. "See, I wanted my dad's gravestone to say, 'This man died of soup.' I wanted my mom's stone to say, 'This woman made it—thinner and thinner.'" He went inside for two bottles, then crossed the alley to visit his friend, Joe Paschowski.

Luke stopped at the pecan orchards. He thought about his mother whose letters from Illinois always added miles to the distance between her and her sons by offering them salvation "at the simple cost of repentance."

He sat against one of the dark, cool trunks and, breathing in, knew he himself smelled like the trees, like dust and dormant green life. He remembered Michael sternly saying, "Go back inside, Dad," and his dad taking the order as if from another adult.

5

At the next level the quiet in the smokestack was even more complete and the sounds of machinery and men below us more unfamiliar. Our jackhammers were muffled like fists pummeling mattresses. The bricks resisted us, coming apart in shards that flew at our feet and ricocheted from the scaffolding pipes. The heat was not much greater than at the first level but was more concentrated in the closer space. Occasionally one or the other of us inhaled deeply to catch our breaths; over the hammers, you could hear the breathing out and in through the masks, like a slight wave licking sand.

Finishing before me, Matthew recoiled his hose and kicked the scaffold floorboards clean. He leaned toward me, craning his neck so I could see him around my hood. He pointed at his watch. I said, "Almost."

He helped me pickax the last of my section of brick. Pointing at the water thermos, he asked, "Now?" It was a horrible sound, that word hissing through his mask. I don't know how to put it down here right, the clear echo that one question still makes in me. I told him to go ahead, but none for me yet. Despite how badly he wanted a drink of it, he wouldn't take any then.

"You've done my work *and* yours," I said. "Take some." But he wouldn't.

We sat again on our coiled hoses; our breathing eased. His safety glasses still on his face, Matthew polished the lenses, then he rolled his shoulders forward and rotated his head in order to loosen his neck.

I said, "Stiff, huh?"

"Plenty."

"You look pretty looney, Matthew."

He had a talent for it. When we were kids he could snake his way out of a whipping with his looney look. In school he invited himself into and out of fight after fight with it. Guarding him in basketball, you never wanted to make eye contact because as soon as you did he looney-looked you and rifled his shot in.

"I've been figuring marketing for The Big Sign. You have to be sensitive you know, Michael." If he was giving me the looney look—I thought maybe he was—I couldn't tell because of the hood and mask and glasses and everything. When he liked you a whole lot, Matthew would give you the looney look to cheer you up sometimes. Or if you wanted to say thanks or congratulations or—worse—that you were sorry, he would spare you the awkwardness by being awkward and looney-faced. It told you he understood. "The Big Sign customers will want to know we're sensitive," he said.

"No problem," I said. "We'll leave the eagle shit—"

"No, not like that. I mean when we make a poster of a car salesman we don't make him too small—even if he *is* too small."

"Right," I said. I was thinking about how much my dad loved us all. About how, after Luke left, when we wanted sometimes (like at the basketball championships or after we all three drank enough) to be feeling how much we loved each other, Matthew would make his grandest looney-look. It told you, Let's hug each other just once, huh? It told you, Nah! My dad (he just came from people who didn't hug, I guess) loved Matthew for that, I know it.

"Michael," my brother said, poised on the coiled hose, "when the Big Sign people get to know you've got good advertising sense, you get job after job I bet."

"Leave us time for farting off, okay?"

"Okay. Okay. But it's a thinking man's business. The car salesman on a sign can't be too small or smile too smug. You see what I mean? He can't have a straw hat or a tan."

"Nobody trusts a salesman with a pretty tan," I said.

"Yeah. Graphics give signals, you know. If you put WILBUR FUNERAL HOME on a sign it has to be big huge letters."

"Right. That says, 'THE END.'" Wilbur Grove Funeral Home was the place that had made arrangements for Dad's funeral.

"Mr. Wilbur can't have a nice tan or a straw hat or horizontal stripes on his suit. Strictly vertical."

"Strictly heavenward pinstripes," I said. "Or just solid. And dark."

His voice more serious, Matthew said, "Mr. Wilbur should be standing below the letters not above them. He should have oily hair and should be pale. And waxy."

"That's great, Matthew. It's perfect. Like he 'relates' to

his customers because he's half-dead himself, but he relates to you too because he can still buy a classy but respectful road poster, can't he?"

"Exactly." He laughed into his gas mask, which made him cough.

When he finished hacking, I said, "Ready?"

He nodded his head yes.

At Dad's funeral home visitation, Matthew had enraged my mother. It had happened after a little Catholic service and after everyone but my mother and us two had gotten into our cars to drive to the graveyard. Just before the coffin was closed, Matthew had leaned over Dad and looney-looked him.

It upset even him that he had done it, I guess, because he started crying and he cried quietly until we came home. It was the next day before my mother could talk to him, she was so mad. She said only, "You . . . a grown man."

•

By Christmas Eve, Marvin was able to walk without stumbling and, Luke also discovered, able to eat plenty at breakfast. Sovel, too, recovered his healthy appetite. The canned soups and boxes of macaroni and powdered cheese which Luke had stockpiled all year would be gone quickly if he didn't send the two men away. No scrap wood was left. When he approached Sovel about helping him find more, Sovel claimed, "It's all I can do is to see for him, Luke," adding indignantly, "Scraps are too much for you to find?"

During Marvin's recovery, Luke planned the day he would get them to leave. He would just say straight out that it had been long enough, right? Right! And you'll be going your way again? Right. He meticulously shaped and shaded in every instant of The Final Good Riddance.

Bye, Marvin—you too, Sovel.

He would shake their hands. He would let Sovel start to prolong the moment but stop him by putting thirty dollars in his hand.

"Okay! Well, all right!" Sovel would say in that meanest way he had of saying thanks.

Bye.

Luke would wave. Nod. And smile too. But not so broad as to completely betray his delight. He would not wave long enough for them to reconsider.

Bye. When Luke turned his back, he'd look one last instant over his shoulder and see them walking away, Sovel counting the money, Marvin still waving. He'd think that Marvin wasn't half bad really. Ducking into the hut, he'd say to himself, Bye then, Marvin.

He'd wonder about Marvin. For a long time, he'd wonder about him. Maybe the rest of his life. Nevertheless, for that first few minutes alone in his hut Luke would smile and smile.

But, when the time came, the perfect, uncomplicated good-bye changed. Walking with them on the narrow dirt road which was the only separation between the pecan orchard and El Cerro, Luke said, "Sovel, what day is it?"

"Huh?"

Luke walked slower. "Hasn't it been long enough?"

"Been a long time for us, too," said Sovel. "Happy we come down?" He guided Marvin around a caved-in section of wire fence.

"I'll be happier when—"

"Well, thanks. Sure's an extra hair up the butt having us here," Sovel said. "And don't we know it? Know it—don't interrupt me now, Luke—and appreciate it, huh, Marvin?"

Marvin nodded.

A smile eroded Sovel's best beholden-to-you expression. Once more Sovel had perfectly anticipated Luke's intentions and expertly held him off. "We wasn't planning on no long stay, anyway, huh?" Sovel said to Marvin, not letting Marvin respond. They followed the road another hundred yards through one of the oldest orchard corners to the river bank.

"Hell, you know it, Luke, we took up with each other, Marv and me, so we'd never need nobody *but* each other.

"Have a sit?" Sovel asked. "Here you go, Marv. Sit down, Luke."

As Luke sat before a dead tamarisk bent over the flat, cold bank, he knew he'd lost. He decided it was better to wait until after Christmas. Or New Year's.

Sovel arranged the greatcoat over Marvin's legs. "It ain't easy for us neither is what I'm saying. Cooped up like we are and you no big conversationalist and Marv here like to get worse before he gets better."

Luke pulled up the hood of his sweatshirt and lay back. He figured it must be nine in the morning. Sovel was talking now about Albuquerque, about how he wondered sometimes if Marvin and Marvin's sister had the same strain of disease, about how these things do run in the genes, don't they? He talked about genes and that led him to talking about women, which led him on and on. "That's tamarack," he said. "They used to call them trees hackmatack," and on and on.

He told how he and Marvin had been busing or hitching from up north down to Las Almas for pecan harvest every year since 1962. "You know they used to do layer hens and little pullets here on Stahmann's farms? You know how birds like nuts? They like the dangdest things."

Luke looked over at Marvin who had slumped onto his side. He covered him better. He touched Marvin's shoulder and then face. His own unaccountable love for the man confusing him, he moved away.

"Geese was here, Luke. Spring and summer. More geese here in these trees then than anywheres else in the world. Cotton farmers up and down this valley bought the goslings for weeders."

Luke said, "Quiet down."

"You don't believe it?" Sovel picked at his nose with his little finger. "You never heard about it?"

"Sovel."

"See? Nobody believes the truth. No need to be truthful in this world, I always say. Because nobody believes." Sovel hooked something and drew it out of his nose. He was pleased.

Luke ignored him and stared up through the tree limbs.

"White Chinese Geese," Sovel whispered hungrily to himself. "All the way from China. Hundreds a thousands."

The sky was a thin layer of dim slate drawing aside for a brighter ceiling. The cold air slowly grew warmer.

On a morning like this in Meltenville, Luke had driven his two brothers across town to the Tractor Lakes. The tiny, rectangular ponds lay parallel, like two unearthly giant Caterpillar tracks, each banked by rotting elms. The swampy weed forest between them was a good place for Michael and Matthew to smoke cigarettes.

They all three sat and looked past their small fire at the thick black moss completely blanketing the water. Michael, almost thirteen, was showing Matthew, three years younger, how to blow smoke through his nose.

Luke didn't smoke. Getting the two little runts out of the house was his job for the morning and he wanted them to know he *wasn't* having fun babysitting them on his day off from the steel mill.

Michael asked Luke if he was still going out with Quiet. He called Luke's girlfriend Loretta "Quiet" because she had come for dinner once and never spoken a word. When Luke didn't reply, Michael said, "Does she *ever* say anything?"

"What does she say?" Matthew asked.

Despite himself, Luke smiled.

"I get it," Michael said. He gave Luke an adult look of understanding that excluded their younger brother.

Matthew said, "I get it too."

"Right." Michael sent two thick tusks of smoke out of his nose. "You bring some beer, Luke?"

"No."

"Too bad."

Michael was in his armor now, head to foot. Guarded by his thirteen-year-old perfected sense of Cool, Michael would say anything, try anything. What a runt, Luke thought. Nevertheless, he recognized Matthew's admiration for Michael and he begrudgingly acknowledged his own weakness in the presence of such Cool. He got out two cans of soda.

Michael mittened his hand around one. He tilted his head

back and guzzled. He crushed it underfoot. When he nodded, Matthew said, "Just a second," and finished his soda with a gulp. "Here." Michael crushed it for him.

"Bet it isn't even cold," said Michael. He pointed an unlit cigarette at the water.

"Yeah."

That was the end of the conversation. They looked at Luke.

Luke wished the little runts weren't so damn sure of themselves. "It's freezing," he said, "and deeper than it looks. And don't get any ideas."

"Yeah?"

"I didn't get an idea," said Michael.

Michael pulled his jacket off. He put the cigarette between his lips. He moved his face near Matthew's. "Light?" He thanked him with a cool nod. "Did you get any ideas, Matthew?"

"Nope."

Talking with their cigarettes dangling from their mouths, they were a funny couple of pygmy tough guys. Luke laughed at them and said, "Swim in that—just even think about it—and I'll break your necks."

Not fifteen minutes later, Michael suddenly plunged—fully clothed, a cigarette in his mouth—into the water. The black moss closed over him.

"Shit!" said Luke. He slowly stood up.

Matthew said, "Did you see that!"

A full ten seconds later Michael's head broke the dark surface a few feet away from them. "Hey!" he shouted. He dragged himself through the moss to the edge of the pond. "Shallow! I knew it!"

The fire they built didn't dry him. It didn't thaw him. They built it bigger. It didn't change the quivering proud grin on Michael's face or the awe in Matthew's eyes.

"You're crazy," Luke said. He forgot that he should break Michael's neck for doing it. He wondered what he should do.

On the drive home in the late afternoon, Luke asked for a cigarette. He lit it, drew on it, gave it to Michael, who already looked ill but simply would not complain. "You're crazy," Luke said.

"Yeah," said Matthew.

Luke offered to turn the car heater up.

"Why?" asked Michael, his teeth clenched.

The tamarisk shivered slightly, drawing Luke out of his daydream. Sovel had talked himself asleep, and the crepey skin of his face and neck had become calm. Even the sweep of his hair drawn over his baldness was unruffled.

Marvin was awake, sitting up, picking away dried mud caked on his shoes.

Luke said, "Hi, Marvin. It must be almost eleven."

"About, I bet."

"You're feeling better?"

"Uh-huh."

Luke had to say it. "I've got to make you guys go in a few days, Marvin."

"Sure," Marvin said. "We're an extra hair up the—"

"Dammit," Luke said, "don't."

"Sorry." Marvin lowered his chin and tilted his eyes up.

The dark skin of his forehead had an angry undersurface.

Luke looked at Sovel, still asleep but murmuring in self-conversation. "He can read me even in his dreams, Marvin. And he'll wake up as soon as he knows I can stand some more."

Marvin said, "Him? Sovel?" They both laughed.

Luke said, "It *is* funny, isn't it?" The air was warmer now. He drew his hands out of his sweatshirt pocket. "Marvin, you've got to stand it all the time. You've had to stand it for—how many years? Twenty?" He was afraid the question he asked next was all wrong. "Why?"

Marvin shifted his legs. "Going to do the trick today?"

"What?"

"The trick."

"I always do one or another on Christmas Eve. At the new mall."

"Can I go?" Marvin asked.

Luke still wanted an answer to his question. He asked it again. "Why?"

Marvin straightened himself to a better sitting position. He looks human again, Luke thought. A man.

Marvin said, "You know how you see a man and a dog alone?" He searched Luke's face. "And they're walking alone. And the dog is on a leash, but he's pulling the man by it. Sometimes, anyway. And it's wrong that the dog is on a leash. Just as wrong the dog wants the leash."

Not sure he understood, Luke nodded.

"Both are alone, right? All alone," Marvin said. "Except for each other."

He tried to stand but needed Luke's help. "Can I go with you for the trick?" he asked.

"Just us two?"

"Okay."

They woke Sovel up and walked back to the hut.

6

Finished with the third level by nine-thirty, we built scaffolding into the fourth. Because of the darkened air above and below us, I couldn't see the rubble we'd knocked down. We each took our second dose of four or five salt tablets before rearranging our equipment around us. The smaller circumference of the smokestack made the heat closer and the quiet absolute. Perfect quiet. Perfect heat. We must've both felt frightened at the very same time because we each mumbled something through our masks. We looked at each other, realized we had caught each other scared.

We couldn't "look" at each other. It's probably better to write that we "pointed ourselves" at each other. The thing is, we had those reflective glasses and silver hoods and hard hats, we stood four inches higher than normal in our wooden-bottom safety shoes, but we—Matthew and I—we could understand the smallest signals in each other's bodies. That's basketball, I guess, the way that you can cock your hips right, lower your left shoulder, point your left temple at a piece of court the size of your palm and, without words, say (very exactly) to your teammate: I'm breaking right and then straight left and if you hit me with a pass *right there* I'm going up under the boards and hooking it in—now!

Matthew and I had that. All the men in my family had that. Maybe it's why we talked so little and got so impatient with awkward talk.

This time we let the quiet be and started stripping the fourth level. The work went slow. Twice my hammer got lodged in the brick and I couldn't extract it until Matthew pickaxed around it. The booze had finally dissolved completely in me and I felt trembly and uneasy. Like before, Matthew put his jackhammer down when he was finished with his work, and he started at mine. He was tired, too. He worked with the same kind of concentration that our dad had eaten meals with. When his drinking was at its worst, Dad would sit before his plate and study the meal like it was an unwanted challenge. At the end, my mother had had to cut his food for him.

At eleven o'clock we were still working on my section of bricks. We hadn't spoken for an hour. I said, "Matthew, we're going slow motion." I suggested we eat our lunches and see if that wouldn't help. He reminded me that the foreman had told us to wait until the sixth level.

"It's two more levels to the sixth," I said.

"Sure is."

"It's Christmas Eve, Matthew! Christmas in another hour!"

"Sure is." He took his mask and glasses off. His long, dark-brown chin hairs were curled tightly upward and looked like an arrow pointing to his lower lip. He looney-looked me.

"Smells like tequila in here," he said, putting the mask on again.

"I'm hungry, Matthew!"

Polishing the lenses of his glasses, he began to hum "Silent Night." As far as I could tell he hummed it until we finished that level. But it might have been his breathing.

Almost done with the last chunk of brick, he stopped. His voice weak, he said, "What'd you get me for Christmas?"

"I'm eating your lunch *and* mine at that sixth level," I said.

"So. What'd you get me?"

I didn't tell him. I looked at my watch. The crystal was completely steamed over, but I thought it must've been midnight. "Merry Christmas," I said.

We sat on our coiled hoses for a long time.

Matthew mumbled through his mask, "Know what I got you, Michael?" Teasing me, he said nothing. "Well?" I didn't bite for it. "I got you a new basketball, Michael. A Voit."

Weeks later, after everything, I ended up sending it, still in the box, to Luke.

.

The sun burnished a patch of gray clouds above them. On the walk to the downtown mall Marvin strode awkwardly, blaming his stumbling on his "dishwasher boots," though clearly something was wrong with his balance. Luke had found that Marvin divided time into the year of the dishwashing job and the present. The bubble-toed hard boots he wore were dishwasher boots because he had bought them "then." He had a pair of dishwasher mittens and a dishwasher stocking cap, which would not fit his head now. He had a beaten-up yellow dishwasher toothbrush with a rubber pick at the end. "I pick every space," he told Luke. The other things he had—a couple pair of pants, a T-shirt and a pullover sweatshirt, a pair of gray wool socks with red toes—"I've had since I stopped growing."

"Yeah?"

"Sixteen, seventeen."

"Before then, what was it—what were you—like when you were little, Marvin?"

Marvin, behind Luke, caught up with him in two imbalanced strides. "Strange question, Luke."

"Oh."

He lagged a step behind again. "I have a good memory. People don't think I would."

"Guess not." Luke glanced back.

Marvin pointed at his temple; he circled his finger there and smiled, and said, "Loco Marvin."

"Well. . . ."

"But." Marvin said softly, "Forget it."

Luke let him catch up. They walked together, saying nothing, then they looked up at each other at the improbable identical instant. Luke wanted to know more. He could see that Marvin wanted to say more.

Marvin said, "Why do I talk to you so much? I never talk so much to other people." He took a deep breath and blew it out loudly. "You tire me out."

"Just anything, then. Tell me just one thing." He watched Marvin's blotched, swollen face.

"One thing." Kicking a piece of bottle glass on the road, Marvin said, "My grandfather was a storyteller. My mother was a listener, and so was I." He hitched his pants up a little.

"My mother could listen, hear anything. I learned from my mother to hear when a snake or a hawk talked to its prey. Things you could never find with your eyes, she heard. When we gave our trees water, she would stand after that, her ear to the trunk. Say it was a poplar—she would make me come and listen to the low groaning. We would go to this other dry poplar and listen. If it was near the drinking poplar, it would groan too, like it knew how good that water tasted.

"One time I got bitten all over my head by ants. I had wanted to listen to them. Some even crawled into the caves of my ears. I hurt bad. All my mother wanted to know is what did I hear?" Marvin repeated the question to himself. "What did you hear, Marvin?" and he laughed.

"There, Luke. One thing."

Luke shook his head. "It's not exactly fair, Marvin."

"No." Marvin raised his head to see Luke better. "You want to know what I heard," he said.

"Well?"

"I heard ants telling stories. Other ants listening."

They cut toward the pecan orchards and walked along the shoulder of old Highway 28, their conversation broken into moments as short as the moments the sunlight burned through breaks in the clouds. At the cotton gin, Marvin asked to stop. Their feet dangling below them, they sat on one of the big wagons in which the cotton is hauled. The dust-blasted white letters on the gin sign were outlined in newly painted red: MESILLA CO-OP GIN ASSN. INC. QUALITY GIN-NING OF UPLAND AND AMERICAN PIMA COTTON.

Marvin gripped the edge of the wagon and slapped the floorboards. "Sovel is not that bad a man," he said.

"What?" Luke asked. "What brought that up?"

"Gin."

"Uh-huh."

Losing his balance as he lay back, Marvin bumped his head. He laughed at himself, and he cursed in another language.

"Who would think it?" Luke said. "I mean, I forget you're Indian sometimes, Marvin."

"Not much of one, Luke. I'm like you. You say you were steel mill people. That's born into you, I think—I don't know—like blood. I'm Antelope Clan. The clan of the cacique leaders," he said. "Your brother's wife, his baby—they're Tewa." He closed his eyes so tightly his face tensed into a wince. "Oh," he said, the faint word compressed with pain.

"Clair?" Luke said. "She's—"

"All Tewa," said Marvin. "Look again at her." He pulled his knees to his chest.

"Are you going to be all right?"

Marvin released his legs like a grasshopper just unboxed. "In a while." Half an hour later, Marvin fished in his pocket for the sleeping pills and pushed them from his palm into his mouth. "That—about blood relations."

Luke scooted from the wagon to the ground. "What is that exactly?"

"Don't know," Marvin said. He took Luke's forearms and eased off the wagon. "We are not our brothers. But I have this feeling like they pull at us in our blood." He lightly tamped his feet on the ground. "You know about that?"

The two men reached the mall late in the afternoon. Marvin was sluggish from the pills he had taken, so he slumped against one of the square brick trash receptacles along the walls of the enclosed mall. By the time Luke drew a crowd, Marvin was half asleep, his head bowed into the flagstones before him. Katherine, Jerry, Dibs, Agnes Sanchez—all the Gospel Rescue Mission regulars came. Every Christmas they came. However, because they knew they were poison to Luke's audience, they stayed a good distance away; they kept their private cheering section quiet, and after his show they left without breaking into the mall crowd to wish him merry Christmas.

After the trick, as Luke passed the coffee cup around, he saw the bicycle lady standing near Marvin, looking down at him curiously. Her dark hair was gathered under a white beret, and she wore the same Christmas-red turtleneck and wool pants. Though he could not clearly see her face through the milling crowd, he thought she was introducing herself to Marvin, who began to wake up, then raised his head a little but was unable to lift it very far. Marvin mumbled something punctuated with a loud snort. Some of the people waiting to give money left; the others dropped their change into the cup and quickly walked away. "Merry Christmas!" Luke said to each one, and "Thanks!" None of them met his eyes, but some had smiled and said, "You too," or "What a trick," or "God bless you"—these last, the very cheapest. He was not above some silly, generous pity and, in fact, it made him happy to do his trick so well that people offered him their loose change and also some of God's. When the last of them had gone, he put the money and cup into his box. He figured he had made twenty-five dollars.

Then, he walked directly toward Marvin and the woman, whose rich brown skin blushed sepia at her neck and cheeks.

She stepped a little away from Marvin as if she had been discovered doing something improper.

"He's okay," said Luke. He bent and put his hand on Marvin's back. "You okay?"

"Me? Sure," Marvin said. He straightened himself a little more.

Luke stood again. He introduced himself as Hoop McWelt. "He's Marvin," he said. "I think the trick puts him to sleep."

"No, no," she said, firmly shaking his hand, "it could not." She looked into his face. It startled him most, he knew, because people just never looked straight at him. But there was something more. Still holding his hand, she looked a question into his eyes: Do you know?

She gave him his hand back and said (he thought she said it more to Marvin than to him), "No." She smiled. "Evenesca Fresqueno, Mr. Hoop. I am happy to meet you." She lowered her head with a slight, graceful movement.

"Thanks—I mean, for coming."

She gazed through Luke at something behind or inside him. He followed her widening eyes but saw just the crowd of shoppers, the mall shops. "So many came to see."

"What?"

"The trick," she said. "The stores almost emptied to see you."

"All—most," Marvin muttered.

Luke asked, "You better, Marvin?"

"Maybe."

"You look better," she said.

Suddenly more certain, Marvin said, "Yes." He tried to get up. She bent low and placed her arms around his waist to help him. When he was up, she kept her arms around him for a moment as she had kept her hand in Luke's. "There." She stepped back from him.

"Evenesca," Marvin said.

"Call me Eva," she said to both of them—and to Luke—"I will see you."

"You have to go?" Marvin asked.

"I have to go a long way home," she said, "like you."

Marvin's eyes lowered. "She said she lives by us, Luke."

Nobody lived near them. Romelia maybe. The chile plant crew at certain times of year. "You live around us?"

"Very near."

"Near the Black Mesa?"

"My mother calls it 'El Cerro.'"

Marvin said, "See?"

"Are you kidding me? Romelia?"

"My mother."

"I'll be damned."

She took his hands up and closed her smooth, dark fingers over them. "She likes you. She says you've been kind to her."

"He *is* a kind of a kind guy," said Marvin.

"So," she said, "I will see you?"

"Yep. Yep. Hope so." Luke sounded silly to himself. Like a clumsy, hopeful boy.

She strode away. "And goodbye too," she said over her shoulder to Marvin. They watched her walk through the Walgreen's and out of the mall.

"Evenesca," said Marvin. He pronounced each syllable in the very same way Luke's mother used to say at church rosaries, "Mother of God, pray for us." He and Michael and Matthew would scoot the beads, like marbles, off their thumbs and solemnly mumble, "Mugod pay us."

Though the veined skin at his cheeks looked bruised, Marvin seemed better. "Can you handle the walk back?" Luke asked, picking up his box of things and his cup of money.

"Maybe."

"We might get a hitch."

7

I had my asbestos pants and work pants and underwear around my knees (no zippers on the asbestos suit) and was concentrating, because I wanted to urinate and the heat wasn't helping. Matthew turned around from his work just about the time I relaxed and felt I could go. "That's a good idea," he said.

"Dammit," I said. He had ruined my concentration.

Instead of going with his back to me, he stood next to me like we were at urinals somewhere, and he pulled down his pants and underwear. He went immediately.

Pulling his clothes back up, he said, "Problems there, Michael?" The look on his face was a half-assed attempt at a looney look.

"I'm better without an audience," I said.

"Oh." He turned away. "Think melting icicles, Michael."

"Come on."

"Sorry."

When I'd finished, he tapped me on the back. I expected some crack about my concentration problems. Instead, he said, "I'd like to shoot some balls in Forest Park next day off. What would you think about that—take a drive out to Forest Park—stop in St. Louis for some beers on the way back?"

"It's—" I started to say it was icy and cold and miserable outside, but that never mattered to either of us. We scraped the snow off courts all winter long and played one-on-one in the windiest, rottenest weather. "Okay," I said.

We went back to work. Almost as if Matthew had planted the thoughts in my mind, I thought about Forest Park and a particular trip we'd taken there with Mom and Dad. Matthew must have been thinking about it. He must have wanted me to think about it with him.

One year, a week after Christmas, Dad had gotten second-degree burns on his back and left shoulder in an accident at the blast furnace. If not for the foul smell of the salve on his burns we wouldn't have known, because he only explained when Matthew, who was about five years old then, asked why he stunk. After he told us, he said it didn't matter anyway, it just meant he had a couple of paid sick days coming and we could maybe make a trip to Forest Park on one of them. We planned it for the very next day.

Matthew and I dove into the Olds ten minutes before Mom and Dad got in. Luke brought his new Christmas-gift place-kick stand and our old football. We made Matthew sit between us in the back seat but he didn't whine for long because that was just never like him even when he was really small.

Dad sat leaning forward to keep his back held away from the car seat. Mom had some great idea that we should sing Christmas songs on the drive. "Hell," he said, "we're not a choir, you know. We're guys out on the town."

"You're boring is what you are," she said.

Eventually, we sang. Luke sang "O Holy Night" with his

nose pinched between his fingers. Dad said, "You want to get crowned?" And Luke stopped.

Driving through Forest Park, we scouted good places to build a snowman. It was early morning and the snow everywhere was deep and untouched. The statue of Saint Louis was laden with it; a funny helmet of snow covered his horse's head. The little lake where the electric boats ran in the summer was frozen over, and its pale green ice tinted the whorls of snow that blew across it. On the other side was the wide expanse of lawn before the Forest Park Opera; we drove through its curved entranceway lined with golden and royal blue and silver banners. Even through the closed car windows you could hear the snicking sound they made in the wind.

We stopped near the tennis courts deeper in the park. The benches outside the high fences were piled up with snow and covered by a layer of elm leaves that had managed to hang on the trees until the worst storms. The basketball courts and open-air handball courts were nearby, and in a small open place between them we tried to build two snow-men. The idea—it was mine—was to build a snowman building a snowman.

Mom was especially terrible at rolling round snowballs; she always ended up with narrow, breakable cylinders. Dad took them from her and said they would make great arms, huh, boys? He winked.

Luke planted his place-kick stand in the snow and set the football in it. Over and over again, he backed up and charged at it and kicked it into the high tennis court fence. Once, Dad went to fetch for him, but Luke said he could do well enough alone.

When we finished, the snowmen looked funny. As it turned out, the one that was supposed to be building the other looked like an unfinished wreck and the one that was supposed to be being built looked pretty good, even headless. Back in the car, we looked at it a final time. Dad said, "Bad arms."

"Yeah," said Luke.

"Let's go to Stix now," said Mom. Earlier, she had asked if we could go there first. By a three-to-one vote she had lost.

We drove to Stix, Baer & Fuller in St. Louis and parked behind the store warehouse. The door we walked in was under a big sign that said, "Damaged Sale." Inside the huge warehouse were furniture and appliances and one whole section of stereos and televisions. We wandered around the warehouse and looked at the dryers with broken windows, the beds with chipped headboards, the stained mattresses. And it really was interesting because it was fun to find out what was wrong. The prices were all still too high, Mom said.

A hi-fi in an elaborate cabinet had a Nat King Cole record playing. He was my dad's favorite, so we sat on a sofa (missing a cushion) near it and listened.

> *The wind blows a kiss through your hair, Annabelle.*
> *But mine is the kiss of despair, Annabelle,*
> *For I am wanting you so—*
> *And you . . . say no. . . .*

We had the album at home and a small record player; I'd heard the songs, knew them by heart. Matthew and Luke did too, so we asked if we could roam around.

When we came back, they were still sitting close together listening, Dad's arm around Mom, her arm hovering over his burned shoulder, her hand and fingers touching the back of his neck, Nat King Cole singing to them from a hi-fi with torn fabric in one speaker.

In the heat and discomfort of the smokestack I could remember absolutely every detail of it. It did not occur to me then to wonder why Matthew wanted me to remember it all.

This last week, writing all this down and trying to make every word of it just right, I've wondered about his reasons all over again.

They really were happy then, Mom and Dad. Dad was not drunk. Mom was not some painted-glass votive candle. They were a part of each other's love; we were an expression of that.

What I think now is that that day was one of the last times Matthew and I remembered seeing them—seeing us—so right.

The scaffolding wouldn't fit together right at the fifth level. One of the pipe sleeves was pinched and wouldn't accept the joiner. We beat open the sleeve with a pickax; we crunched the end of the joiner pipe; then the fit was too loose, so we attacked them again. We worked for at least half an hour on the damn pipe arms.

"Break?" Matthew asked.

"We shouldn't right now," I told him. It was beginning to worry me that we'd already spent so long.

"Come on, Michael."

I moved a little closer to him. "You all right?"

"Look, what's the big deal? What's the big deal about a five-minute break?"

I explained that we were running real late already. I should have taken his mask and hood and hard hat off and looked at him. If I'd paid attention, I could have known how bad he needed a rest. "We'll be finished in a little bit," I said.

We started again on the scaffolding. We talked a while. When Matthew stopped, I continued. I got some kind of strange comfort from our voices, my voice. The words were like ballast I could spill to keep gradually rising out of that smokestack like some kind of hot-air balloon. So, I talked into my mask and sometimes I lost my breath or even gasped or waited for Matthew to say something, but I talked and talked and talked the whole time we worked.

I'm not sure what I said exactly. Anyway, I shifted back and forth, like I do, from things I'd already said to things I shouldn't say, until pretty soon we almost had the scaffolding assembled.

I shouldn't, for instance, have mentioned Irene. Irene was a looker, a bookstore owner's daughter, and she'd always seemed crazy about Matthew. She didn't like his drinking and she didn't appreciate, either, his wanting the sign-painting business since I guess she knew she wasn't included in our plans.

Because of both things, she didn't much care for me. They fought a lot, broke up a lot, this latest breakup just one of many. I liked her all the same—a bookstore owner's daughter who hated books, a smart-alecky Midwestern girl.

"Are we going to take Mom out to dinner New Year's Eve?" I asked. Matthew was slowly hauling equipment up to the fifth level. He had ignored me for almost half an hour. I said, "You got plans then?

"No? Well, it's a shame because you know Mom. She'll—"

"I know," he said. He began to coil his jackhammer hose.

"She'll bitch about drinking and holler about Dad and plan our funerals if we don't quit, and promise to kill us if we do quit and dare start again."

Lifting the two pickaxes up and resting them at his sides, he leaned down. "You can come up," he said. He put his hands over my forearms, but gripped them too weakly to be any help.

"It's okay."

"Sorry," he said.

"All right. Sit down, Matthew. But just for a minute."

He sat with his elbows resting on his knees; he hunched over, his big hands barely folded and pointed downward so that they looked like some large bird diving with its wings folded back. Benched for a few minutes in a basketball game, he would do the same thing. During sermons in church, the same thing. My dad held a bottle that way. When I think hard, I see it a hundred times: Matthew's head bowed a little and his shoulders hunched slightly. The position made his body a question mark. What to do with these hands? he seemed to ask.

·

L uke and Marvin took a shortcut past the cotton gin and through the southwestern corner of the pecan or- chards. At sunset the rock spines of the Sierra de la Soledad were the pulsing orange of cooling ingots and, all around, the trunks of the bare pecan trees were nearly as dark as the last shadows disentangling themselves on the damp earth. Marvin stopped. "What is that?" he said.

"What?"

"From there."

They moved cautiously a little closer to the reed-hidden hut, and then Luke heard it too. Someone mumbling or humming. A sound he recognized. "Her music."

"We can listen."

Luke said, "Sure," understanding that Marvin meant they should stop before walking through the reeds so they could listen. They stood close to each other, as if hearing would be easier that way.

"Okay?" Marvin asked, enclosing Luke's fists inside his own cold hands. Marvin shifted his chin down and turned his head so that it inclined toward Ruth's singing; he glanced down at their overlapping fingers.

Luke accepted the unspoken invitation for him to do the same. He felt his fist warming inside Marvin's. His palms wanted room; his fingers needed to unfold, but Marvin would not let them. When Ruth's chanting stopped, Luke had to push his hands up and out of Marvin's, closed like the halves of a seed pod.

If Marvin had said anything, any harmless single word, Luke would have felt shame for holding hands with another man. "Marvin," he asked, "is that some ritual or something?"

"No." Marvin bit at dirt under his thumbnail. "Felt good."

They pivoted apart and stepped through the reeds. "Ruth?" Luke called. He saw her sitting outside with her back against the hut wall.

"Shhh," she said, lifting one arm from around the child. "She's asleep."

"How'd you get here?"

"A longer walk than we thought," Ruth said. "Clair got cold."

Marvin crouched down near her. "Please," he said, and Ruth lifted the child into the cradle of his arms. He rearranged the blanket around her. "I've got her. You two go ahead, okay? Talk." He nodded at Luke, then took Clair inside.

Ruth pulled the hood of her coat around her face. "Michael doesn't know what he's doing," she said, "or even where he's at sometimes. I couldn't be there. But I didn't want to be that far from him."

"Michael? What's he done? What do you mean?"

"His sickness—his drinking—it's been worse." She spoke evenly, raising her head and then lowering it again. "He's like a helpless child."

"What happened? When—when did this happen?"

She shook her head, as if to say that was a question which should not be asked. "He frightens Clair."

"Dammit, tell me. Come on. We were together a week ago."

"That was when you brought the two men."

"Look," he said, "I know about drunks. They don't lose it like that." He couldn't keep back the lie which he hadn't even known he owned. "I tell you what, they don't go scaring their kids—not because of one weird night."

"He sits at the typewriter. He has not gone to work. He has not eaten unless I beg him to."

"Well, he's sick."

"He doesn't sleep."

"He's had a little lapse. Ruth, you can't run out on him, can you?"

"His face is different." She lowered her head once more. "He says he's working something out. It's all he says." Her tears wet her long, unbound hair. "Everything will be all right, he says, if he can just work something out."

"This is tough for him, the Christmastime. You know that." Luke had been kneeling near her, but now he sat back on his heels, his knees near her waist.

"In seven years he's never been like this," she said.

He started to say again that it was a lapse; she could give Michael the benefit of the doubt, couldn't she? But those wouldn't have been *his* words.

"Ruth, I'll go see him. You watch. I'll get him straight." The conviction in the words melted as he said, "It's a mess, I know, and I'm not helping any. I can't believe it, is all."

He helped her to her feet and walked her into the hut. Marvin was huddled over Clair, who was singing so softly Luke could not be sure he wasn't just imagining the strange music. "Take care of them, Marvin," he said. "I have to go see my brother."

"Luke, Sovel's gone. Look. He left us this." Marvin handed a piece of paper to Luke.

Luke stuffed it into his pants pocket. "I'll help Michael," he said to Ruth. He hurried over the bridge on the irrigation ditch and through the dark orchard and over two stripped fields, then on to Main, where Michael and Ruth's trailer was parked behind the El Don Motel. He stood one block from it, and watched the Villa Motel sign light up very briefly, darken for a long time and light up again so briefly there was no afterimage.

Remembering the note from Sovel, he pulled it from his pocket.

> Marv—Luke,
> Got business to look into.
> See to each other now.
> —S

He shoved the paper back into his pocket and stood before the flimsy trailer door. He knocked. For Sovel, "business" meant he was gone and probably meant it had been his plan from the start to dump Marvin and disappear. *You,* Luke thought, *You*—but no word was black enough to satisfy him.

8

I looked at my useless watch. "Think it's still snowing outside?"

"Maybe," he said. "I wonder if T.A.'s all right."

"You worry about him, huh?"

"Yeah. . . ."

We were going to talk about him, I could tell; I don't know why I cut us short. "Look out," I said.

"Okay," said Matthew, "all right."

"I worry about him too."

"Need some salt?" Matthew asked.

"And lime. And a margarita."

"Waiter!" Matthew hollered. "Waiter!" Only the first syllable made it through the mask. It rang off the close walls and fell, clanged in the bottom of the smokestack, and rebounded with an echo that gained force as it rose through us and then out the top.

We both, like clappers in a bell, we both hollered it: "Waiter!" but it came out, "Wait!"

"Lousy service," he said, and handed me some salt tablets he drew from his jacket pocket. He didn't take any.

When we lifted our jackhammers again, he went back to singing some Christmas tune, but between the muffled gatling sounds of the machinery I couldn't make it out. The walls were so close that we sometimes bumped back to back. Neither of us turned around. Once, the backs of our hard hats hit with a dull clunk, and we glanced at each other's metal/asbestos/glass faces. But there was no point in talking. I think we both felt talking would be a risk at that stage. We were hungry and weak. I thought if I didn't admit to him that I was also nauseated, it would help us keep the funny balance we'd found. Although Matthew was always stronger than I, I suspected he was feeling sick too. His stupid Christmas caroling was a way of hiding that.

The lantern we had with us was more and more useless. Our safety glasses too. Even continuous blinking brought no moisture to my eyes.

This time I finished my section before Matthew, and tried to help him. It was impossible to fit safely next to him, so I had to wait until he shifted his body just a certain way before I could fit my jackhammer behind and to the left of his. In a few minutes his shifts and feints were second instinct to me and when he pivoted a certain way I antici- pated the move. Just before we finished off the last bricks, he faked a pivot one way and moved another. I could barely hear his mumbling beneath the mask, but I got the message and quit to let him finish by himself.

·

M ichael opened the door. "Hoop."
   "Let me in?"
"Sure, Hoop." Michael stepped back. "Did they go to you? Is that where they are?"

"They're with me—with Marvin." Luke could not tell whether Michael was drunk.

"I'm almost finished. I'm so close." His voice weak, he said, "I told her how close I was; she didn't have to . . ." He leaned against the partition between the kitchen and bedroom of the small trailer.

"What's this about? What are you doing, Michael?"

"I'm getting it down on paper, Luke. I'm getting it all down so I can see it straight. Don't look at me like I'm some—like I'm boozed."

"Well?" Luke said.

"I haven't been drinking since I started this, Luke. I haven't drunk much." He sat on the couch, sank into it, then straightened. "A little."

"You're sure *acting* goddamn crazy. What about your jobs?"

Michael looked past him. "I have to do this."

"Right, Michael. Right." The space heater set up in the kitchen entrance was on too low. It hummed and rattled and gave no heat.

"I told them I only needed a little more time. I'm close to finishing. I told them. Ask Ruth. Ruth knows what they said to me."

"This is crazy."

"I quit! They didn't fire me! Did she tell you that?" Michael sat down. He kneaded his legs with his hands. "Please, Luke, I just want to see everything straight."

"It's Matthew then?"

"Luke, I need a little more time."

Luke sat on the couch next to Michael. He thought about how odd his brother's eyes were, how unusual, in fact, all the McWelts' eyes were. The short, irregular stubble of their dark eyebrows was probably the reason, he guessed. Or the fact that they almost had no eyelashes. In one job or another at the mill, their lashes had been singed off and had only partially grown back; as a result, their eyes always had that just-startled look of infants.

Luke spoke quietly at first. "It's freezing in here. It stinks." He felt the current of his own voice pull him under. "It smells like a man's been locked up here building a—digging a hole for a man who's been dead eight years."

Michael stood. "No. Jesus, no. You don't know. Are you stupid? Don't you—don't call it that." He went to his typewriter, pulling himself close to the edge of the table on which it rested.

"What are you making then? Some kind of comic book? Michael, you know what you're doing?"

"I'm not a hobo, for Christ's sake! I'm not a street bum like my big brother, am I?"

"No."

"I don't—look at you, Luke. What's to look at in me that's worse? You make me sick with shame. You know that?" He lightly touched the table edge as if gauging its sharpness. "No? You know it."

"So. You act like you have to bank everything on this, Michael. The works."

Michael folded his large hands over the typewriter and rested his chin on them. He closed his eyes. "It's a trick, Hoop. You bank everything on the ball landing on the yard-stick and staying. Dad banked everything on a job he hated, right? Mom bets everything on God's—on His what? Mercy? Matthew and I, we thought if we could make a little more money. . . . I need just this. I'm almost over."

Luke had forgotten Michael could have such innocent determination. All their adult lives he had known the drunken Michael, the man like their father.

"Tell me this—swear it—that you haven't had anything to drink."

"Not since just after I started."

"So, what do I do, Michael? Leave the soldier in his bunker? Make you shower and sleep and bring you food when you need it so you don't get sick?"

Raising his head, Michael looked at the small stack of typewritten pages to his left. "I never thought of that before, Hoop."

"What?"

"How far does the Cyrenian help Jesus? In the stations, when he helps Jesus, does he help him all the way? Well? Well, it doesn't say, does it?"

Luke shouted, "You're not Jesus, for Christ's sake!" At almost the same time, as they both realized what he had said, they began to smile.

"For Christ's sake!" said Michael. "That's good."

"The Stations of the Cross." Luke walked to the space heater set up at the kitchen entrance. It was so small he knew it would be useless even if he turned it up higher. "Look, Michael, how much longer will this take?"

"A few days. A week."

Luke shook his head.

Michael said, "I'm not Jesus, for Christ's sake." He grinned. When Luke looked away, he said, "Doesn't work twice, huh?"

"No," Luke said. "Hey, at least put on a sweatshirt or a coat or something. You got food? Well?"

"Some."

"Eat it, then."

"Okay, Luke. I promise."

"I'll get some of Ruth and Clair's things."

"I'll do that."

As Michael placed stuffed animals and clothing and diapers into a box for Clair, he asked, "How's the big guy?"

"Marvin? He's getting worse."

"His partner?"

"Gone."

"Naturally. So, you're Marvin's new partner?"

Luke thought about that a moment. It made him angry, for some reason, that Michael even asked. "No," he said.

"Clair liked him—the big guy. Just like *that* she liked him. He scared me. But I liked him."

Luke said, "Me too."

"Will he make it?"

"Probably not."

Michael put the two boxes for Ruth and Clair on the small kitchen table. "Tell him I said hi or something."

Luke avoided Michael's eyes; he looked, instead, at the small Coors waterfall clock on the wall above the kitchen range. In the complete stillness of the room, he heard the fluid movement of the clock's mechanisms. "It's past one," he said.

"Here." Michael lifted the boxes into Luke's arms. "Tell them I love them, Hoop. Make them believe I love them."

When he returned to the hut, Luke made a concoction of pinto beans, ham spread, and canned corn. His favorite holiday dinner, he explained. Everyone seemed to enjoy it, especially Marvin, who ate ravenously, with his face close to the bowl. Ruth made coffee afterward and they went inside to drink it.

"Cold out," said Marvin as he sat down.

Luke put his bowl next to him and warmed his folded hands between his legs. "You're right, Marvin," said Luke, "it's that off-the-bare-desert cold."

Clair said, "Bear?" Marvin growled, and he set his cup down to make room on his lap for her.

Luke looked at it all: Clair with her arms branched around Marvin's sides; Ruth holding her coffee close to her face and breathing in the steam; his hut strewn with Ruth's blankets and Marvin's bindle rags; a corner where Ruth had neatly folded and covered her and Clair's underclothes, another corner that had become a messy but warm hibernating place for Marvin. "Beautiful," he said.

Ruth looked a question at him.

"This," he said. "My place, a kind of home. Eating dinner with other folks here."

Marvin shifted position but could not seem to make his neck and head comfortable against the hut wall. Luke said, "Why don't you lie down, Marvin?"

With Clair still in his arms, Marvin slumped onto his side. "Thanks, Luke."

Clair said, "Bear. Growl." Marvin snored like a quiet bear might snore, and the sound soon put the child to sleep.

No one had spoken for a long while when Marvin, his eyes closed, said, "A shame Sovel couldn't be here tonight, Luke."

"Yeah," said Luke, laughing at the thought and then laughing at the strange real appeal of having Sovel there.

Ruth put her cup down. She went to Marvin and the child and covered them with a blanket. She kissed Clair's cheek and Marvin's swollen forehead and sat near them, singing with prayerful concentration, rocking her shoulders and head. When Luke left the hut an hour later, Ruth was still singing.

He had decided to give into it, the constant thinking about Eva. At a place where the moon made a smoky silver blade of itself on the Rio Grande, he sat and talked to her. "What is it?" he said to the cold light on the water. "You want something. What?"

A few minutes before daylight, Luke walked south up the ditch bank to the place opposite Romelia's bee boxes. Each year after Thanksgiving she painted her bee boxes, her front door and her window frames the same color. This year she had painted some of the boxes light blue and others a barely-blue bright white; she must have had paint left over because her two porch posts and her mailbox were also done.

When Romelia answered the door she gripped Luke's upper arm in order to pull him inside. She shut the front door. "It's him," she said, tightening her grip, leading him to the kitchen in the back.

Eva said, "Hi, Hoop." She was cutting a dark brown loaf that smelled like pumpkin bread.

"Hi."

"Mama, you can give him his arm back."

"Or," said Romelia, "I can keep it. You will have breakfast, Mr. Hoop. We have Cream of Wheat."

"Will you?" asked Eva.

He could hardly refuse. Everything seemed so ready for him that he guessed they must have watched him staring at the bee boxes and the house before he had gotten enough courage to knock.

The bowls Romelia set out on the low, hand-carved table were some he had brought to her, a gift from Mr. Zoeller at Albertson's Market. They had the word *Value!* imprinted in pale green along the edges and linked into a circle at the bottom. On the center of the table were two matching Value coffee cups filled up with tiny cotton balls.

Romelia took the pot from Eva and spooned Cream of Wheat into his bowl. She brought honey from a cabinet and opened the jar for him.

As Eva sat down across from him, she asked, "You're going to stay, Mama?"

Romelia said, "Too big for our table. Look at him." She then followed her own advice and looked closely at him, her eyes eventually focusing, as far as he could tell, on his mouth or lips.

This made him eat nervously; it compelled him to say something. "I like hot food in the—"

"Yes," said Romelia.

"—in the morning."

"You have come to court, Mr. Hoop."

"What?" Luke said. "Whoa." He glanced across the table

at Eva, who broke a piece of pumpkin bread from her slice and ate, comfortably watching him.

Romelia chuckled. "This is true. You want to court."

Eva brushed crumbs from her blue jeans, caught them in her left hand, then sprinkled them over her cereal.

Her mother glanced at her. "I can watch?" She saw some kind of answer in Eva. "No?"

"No, Mama."

Her bowl in her hands, Romelia said, "Advice, Mr. Hoop: she is forty-four years."

Luke stared, pretending incredulity. "Thanks," he said. "It helps to know that."

Closing the door behind her, then looking through the back-door window, Romelia slowly nodded her head, the kind of gesture a bird will make when it is swallowing.

"She likes you," Eva said.

"Me too."

"She is stronger than either of us, both of us." Eva had her mother's way of barely but continuously lifting and settling her shoulders and head so that her body and face seemed eager to express what her eyes meant. "So," she said. In her left hand, her long, slender thumb touched the inside of each finger.

"So. So, Eva," Luke said, "am I supposed to commence courting?"

"You are not too good at this, Luke."

"No kidding." Luke weighed the cereal in his spoon. "I never learned the moves." He put the spoon back in the bowl. "If I . . . you're a—you know, pretty."

"I know I am."

"I *would* court you, I think."

Eva leaned toward him. "Be careful. She is watching."

Romelia stood in her garden, hands in her dress pockets, eyes poised to intercept him. *No,* her finch-quick eyes said, *I am not watching very much.*

When he looked again at Eva, her transparent brown eyes, her grin-verging-on-laughter made him think of the word "lovely." If the word means confounding, he thought, then it means the right thing.

"Would you like more?" she asked.

"I would. The pumpkin bread. I'd like some of that."

She cut a thin slice, much thinner than the piece she was eating, and brought it to him. "You see these?" she said picking up one of the tiny cotton balls. "Bee stingers." She brought her chair next to his. Luke could smell the adobe dust and sugary pumpkin scent in her hair. "Her hands hurt her from arthritis. She stings them—her joints."

"That helps?"

"Probably not. You know what I think?" As he was about to pick up the pumpkin bread, she touched his fingers with hers. "I think she stings herself to show her hands how mad she is when they hurt her."

When Luke slipped his arm around Eva's shoulder, he sensed Romelia's instant attention. "Eva," he said, "we *could* court. If you wanted."

She shifted herself, lowering her head to touch the back of his hand with her chin.

Whoa, he thought.

But his heart eased open when he saw Eva mouth the word *Look* to her mother, who mouthed back the words *Oh, Eva.*

9

"Whoa! Shit!" I heard Matthew scream behind me. I was too slow to catch him, and he almost fell through the scaffolding.

"Matthew!"

His jackhammer thudded next to him. He lay on his stomach, heaving. I hollered his name again, but he didn't answer. I grabbed the lantern and crouched with it near his head. "Matthew? Hey!" I tried to turn him over but the equipment everywhere around him made that impossible. Cupping his chin, I turned his head. I pulled off his helmet and said into his ear, "Matthew, are you—what happened? Are you all right?" He shifted his weight. He was breathing more easily. I took his mask off to see if his face was hurt.

His smile opened like a camera shutter and closed as quickly.

"What the hell!" I shouted. I felt as though my skin had jumped off me and landed back all out of place.

He had to remove his eyeglasses to wipe the tears his laughter made at the corner of his eyes.

That's what I saw—the streaks the tears made on his sooty face. That was all I saw. And it angered me so much I couldn't laugh.

"You're sitting on my chest," he said. I threatened to kick it in if he ever pulled that kind of thing on me again.

"Okay, okay. Get off me." His laughter faintly echoed in the smokestack. If I had listened, I would have heard what I hear now: a weak, lying laughter, the kind I sometimes heard myself make into an empty glass.

I got off him and stood up. He raised himself slowly to his knees. He stayed kneeling a long while before he stood.

Now I see them differently, those tears. They make me want to try again, to try and figure out my family.

You can move a mountain if you've got even as much faith as a mustard seed—you can tear a mulberry tree out of the earth and make it root in the sea—the Bible says. The damn book says precious little about the kind of hope that lifts you out of your bed for the midnight shift and burns day in and day out with a blowing flame that draws on all of you for fuel: your pride, your tempered will, your untempered love. Your faith. And it settles all its growing and weakening heat on that—your faith. It rekindles and then smothers it over and over again.

You come home at eight in the morning and your house is emptying out, children going off to school. Your wife— she knows she is only fuel you will use up—wanting to be with you but wanting out too, anxious to drive the car, turns the kitchen radio off and takes a shower, a short one in order to leave you a bath of hot water. And, after the bath, the towels and the bedsheets smell (in the windy part of summer, like high corn and harvested alfalfa; in the stillest part of winter, like smog, like the steel in the machine dryer) like the soot in your throat. Your kids call goodbye, your wife says she'll be back after mass. How to describe her voice? A breath in a shallow cup.

You hear the car crank up, jolt away, and you don't hear another thing in the whole house or around it, not another thing in the whole goddamned world. That—that silence— is the stupid answer to your hope. And you push your face deeper into the heat of the pillows, and try not to, not to, not to. But you fall asleep.

I'm beginning to understand, Dad.

We called goodbye from the front door. Mom said, "He needs it quiet." And we thought being quiet, going away, was loving you.

■

It was still early when Luke returned to the hut. He lay down, taking off his sweater and drawing it over his shoulders and neck like a blanket.

Ruth was asleep on her back. Her knees up, she had covered herself with a blanket and left only her head and feet out. Luke remembered when Michael had first mentioned Ruth Walalata. He had come to Bogel's Deli after Luke's trick and offered to take him inside for coffee.

"Can't," Luke said.

"We'll just have one cup," Michael said. "Have a cup with me."

"Bogel has rules. No hobos. No drunks."

"I'm a working man."

"So am I—in my way."

"Well, goddamn him then, Luke." Michael reached into his pocket for change. He walked into Bogel's and, in a few minutes, returned with coffee. He handed one of the styrofoam cups to Luke. "I've got some news."

"Good?"

"I hate this kind of cup. Like pressed lint."

"Okay," Luke said. Michael had always done that, played that trick. He'd say, "Mom says she needs to talk to you," and then say, "You're probably *not* in trouble. Did you see that labrador the neighbor's got?"

"I'll tell you." Michael led them across Main Street to the railroad tracks. They sat on an elevated section where they could look at Bogel's and, behind the deli, at the reflective gray teeth of the mountains and the few rent webs of cloud above Bishop's Cap.

"Luke, her name's Ruth. Ruth Waves Tossing." Michael tore open another little envelope of powdered cream and emptied it into his coffee.

Luke knew Michael was not going to say another word unless he asked him to. The way it was in the McWelt family was that, in the midst of saying nothing, they said more; on the way to saying something, they stopped short.

"Good."

"She's Indian." He stirred the powdered cream into the coffee with his fingertip. "She's a photographer for the paper."

"Oh," Luke said.

"How's your coffee?"

"Okay, I guess."

Michael balanced the cup on his right palm. "I love her."

That had been all. Luke had started to congratulate him but Michael looked at Luke with an expression that was hauntingly looney. "Know what she says, Luke? She says she chooses me. I can take all the time *I* want deciding because she's already 'chosen me.'"

Two weeks later, Michael introduced Ruth as his wife.

Now, she was asleep in Luke's hut, her lips trembling slightly and, under the blanket, her arms and hands shifting, reaching for something and, losing it, reaching again.

In the left corner at the rear of the hut, Marvin lay coiled around Clair, who perfectly fit the nest his body formed. Like a burrowing owl preparing to go underground, Marvin had driven his forehead into the dirt at Clair's feet. Luke took a deep breath. The talcum smell of the child and the fresh-clay smell of the woman filled the room. He lay down across the floor just inside the hut entrance, shifting his shoulders and head to be near Clair. Sleep came quickly.

The businessmen standing around Bogel's stamped their feet and slapped their gloved hands, resisting the cold weather. The movement became a nervous patting, then a jerking. The jerking turned into a bouncing. The wind was colder and colder. The men curled themselves more tightly inside their leather jackets until the seams of their clothing sealed around them. Then, the human basketballs shivered one final time. Little patches of silver hair or shoe sole or crisply ironed shirtsleeve disappeared into black Voit seams.

In a panic, they dribbled themselves wildly. They slammed and bounced against the asphalt. Flying into the granite winter sky above Las Almas, they drummed against the cloud walls, thundered viciously, and charged away over the fallow chile and cotton farms of Mesilla. The dogs on Fred Huff's farm squealed like pigs as the cold palm of shadow gripped and released the land. Over the Stahmann pecan orchards, past San Miguel, La Mesa and La Union, on then to Anthony, the full-court drive of the clouds continued. They darkened even the foul air above the Asarco smelter in El Paso. Then Mexico.

"Qué maravilloso," a voice said.

Two hands captured his hands and lifted them behind his head, sinking them into thick, coarse woman's hair. Her chin atop his left shoulder, she said, "Mr. Hoop."

"Eva?" he said.

He sat up and looked around him.

Ruth was holding Clair. "Where's Marvin?" Luke asked.

"Outside."

"Ruth, are you all right?"

"You saw Michael?"

"I'll be back in a minute and tell you all about Michael."

He found Marvin splashing water from the river into his face and over his head and neck.

"Marvin, maybe you ought to wash your shirt out."

"Good morning, Hoop." Marvin untucked his heavy work shirt, pulled the long tails close to his face to smell them. He tucked the shirt back in and, smoothing it along his sides, he said, "Wrinkled."

"It smells too."

"I get dirty when I sleep. Sovel says only an Indian can get dirty when he's sleeping." Marvin leaned down, and gathering up the coat at his feet, he dried his hands on the lining. He frowned at them.

"Marvin, you think he'll come back?"

"No."

"You knew he was going to do this?"

His voice like a small bell, Marvin said, "Yes."

Luke wanted to be angry but couldn't be. "It was a stinking thing to do, Marvin."

"I—he told me in Albuquerque. He told me all the time."

"The son of a bitch."

"I didn't believe him. Sovel lied sometimes."

Luke laughed at the ridiculousness. "*Some*times!"

Marvin gritted his teeth against the pain his own laughter caused in his head. "I will tell you something, Luke. It was different." He sunk his hands into his pockets and lowered his shoulders. "My sister, Telopa, and him had a baby like Clair. When that baby died, Telopa left Sovel. I liked him and I wanted to help him—Telopa, I don't know where she went— and so I took care of him. We went on the bum together.

"I had something wrong. My head was so I couldn't get balance. But I took care of *him* a long time."

"Well," said Luke, "he lied about all that too."

Marvin said, "Can we walk back?"

"Okay. Now?" Luke supported him as they walked.

"It was different, what you saw. We took care of each other. Always was that way."

"I don't care," Luke said, "you know that? I don't care. He's still a son of a bitch."

"Always," Marvin said, fondly.

In the late morning, Marvin, Ruth, and Clair left to steal pecans from an isolated corner of the orchards fronting El Cerro. Luke examined the box of tricks he would bring to Bogel's customers in another hour. He palmed the basketball, turned it over in his hand, and thought how high up he had sent his faith; when it had come back to him, he had made a game of sending it back up, high up and far from him. He put the basketball into the box.

He said her name aloud: "Evenesca Fresqueno." I like your name, he said to the image of her made clear within him. "Hell of a name." He pulled Sovel's note from his pocket. He read it again.

10

The brick dust thickened in the air. It formed oblique, wavering curtains that circled us and held our shoulders and backs, then fell away.

Matthew pelleted me with a handful of the junk collecting on our scaffold floorboards. He lowered his jackhammer. "Hey," he said through his mask. When I turned around, he'd lifted his jackhammer again and I figured he hadn't been talking to me. Probably to himself or to his equipment. We both had gotten into the habit of that.

A few minutes later, he sprayed me with a heavier blast of dust. I didn't turn around. I shouted above my jackhammer, "You're such a goddamn little kid, Matthew."

"So," he said.

"Huh?"

"So, what'd you get me for Christmas, Michael?"

"See what I mean?"

"It's Christmas, isn't it? Come on. I told you what I got you."

"Sucker."

We put our equipment down. Matthew handed me a pickax and he took up a broom. When he swept dust onto my back, I said, "Don't push your luck." That was stupid, pretending to be tough. I always sounded unconvincing even to me.

He kept sweeping dust over me. "Think Mom's going to like the tablecloth?" he asked.

"Quit that."

He swept some dust into his hand. "It's way too big. But nice, don't you think?" He dumped the dust onto my shoulders.

I was determined not to cave in. "You got to be Mom to like it, that's for sure," I said. The tablecloth we had bought her for Christmas was red and had green-and-white lace crosses sewn along the borders. It could've hung on an altar.

"Why am I picking and you sweeping?" I asked.

"You need the exercise."

I kicked crud from the nose of the pick. "Matthew," I asked, "what do you think of her?"

"What? Mom?"

"You think she's nuts?"

He held a handful of dust over me. He changed his mind. "God, what a question, Michael."

"Well?"

"I've got to sit a minute."

I finished chipping clean that section of smokestack throat. "Well?"

"She's a nut or a saint, one of the two." He bowed his head, brushed his sleeve across the lens of his glasses.

"Yeah."

"Does it matter, you think?"

"Matthew," I said, "it's more than I can think about."

He asked me to help him off with his asbestos jacket.

"What are you doing?" I asked, undoing the fasteners at his back.

"The thing's binding me or something. My chest feels funny."

Mom, I think you were more saint than nut.

What was it you made me read aloud—because I refused to memorize it—every new Saint's Day, at my first communion, my confirmation, every birthday? Each time we had a fight.

I needed to memorize it, you said.

•

Two days after Christmas, Luke visited Michael again and brought him groceries. They talked only a few minutes, Luke asking him if he was eating. Michael said, "Sometimes."

"Drinking?" Luke asked.

"Milk." He opened a cabinet in his desk. "Nothing. Look, I'm not drinking, that's the truth."

Michael asked about Ruth and Clair. Rummaging around the house, he said, "I forgot to give you Clair's string mittens, Luke. She likes them. She puts them on her dolls and stuffed animals. On the sink handles sometimes." From a kitchen drawer he produced two dirty pink crochet mittens connected with kite string. "Here."

Luke took them. "I'll go."

"You'll tell Ruth, Luke? It isn't long."

"I'll tell her."

"Is the Indian okay?" Michael asked.

"He can talk again, anyway."

"That's good, huh?"

"Maybe."

Michael took the door handle and turned it, but let it go. "Have I ever shown you my hands?"

"Your hands?"

Michael lifted Luke's hands and placed his own, palms up, in them. They were welted with crossed lines of scar tissue.

"Michael, how'd—"

"I'd forgotten about them. Can you believe a guy can wash and shave himself and touch his family with such ugly things and forget? Hard to believe." He took his hands out of Luke's. "I'm remembering things, Luke. Things are coming back to me I shouldn't ever have forgotten."

"About Matthew."

"All of us." Michael opened the trailer door.

Luke said, "Walk some of the way with me."

"Real soon, okay?"

Luke pushed Clair's mittens into a pants pocket. "Bye, then."

"No. Luke, wait a second. I wrote something—I figured out something." On the small trailer porch, Michael was standing close and a little crouched, as if guarding him on court. "You were wrong about leaving for New Mexico."

"I'm going."

"You thought Dad wanted that—for us to go away, let him have some quiet."

Luke said, "Michael, he was a drunk. How would he know what he wanted?"

"He didn't want that." Michael backed away from him. "Go ahead then."

Luke stepped down from the porch. As if to follow, Michael

stepped down also. He shouted, louder and sharper than Luke had ever heard him, "What the hell did he want from us?"

Glancing back, Luke saw Michael's hands raised to his chest, his knees bent, as if he were ready to shoot a long shot.

"You know it, too, don't you?" Michael shouted.

Luke stopped, turned. "Shoot or shut up."

"What?"

"I said—" Luke bent his head into the wind. "Michael," he muttered to himself, "come on. Don't."

"All that hope we gave him. He *had* that, Luke. He had that all by himself some time or other. Before the booze. Before you quit the university. Before Paschowski—and God— always butting in on him and Mom." Each word was like dry wood cracking under a boot. "And then I—Matthew and I—when you and Dad couldn't take any hope from us, we took it from each other. Luke?"

"I'm here, all right?"

"We took it away from each other."

"I'll be back, Michael."

Michael was a faint sound behind him. "Do you see? Matthew might've wanted out. He did."

At the hut, Marvin was riding Clair on his shoulders. Ruth was sitting on the ground nearby, giving Clair instructions. "Tell him to go left. Go right. Slow down!" Marvin clopped his hands against the ground. "Let him drink, Clair."

"Laplaplap!" went Marvin. He lowered himself so Clair could climb off his huge shoulders. She pointed to his belly. It was her signal. Luke sat down next to Ruth.

"A story?" Marvin said. "A coyote story?" He yipped and

howled and bared his teeth. He sat up and made a place for her to sit in his lap. "Coyote."

As if to discover something there, Marvin pushed his hands through the dust at his sides. He took up a handful and pretended to throw it up into the air. Clair giggled when he showed it to her. "Still there," he said. He returned the dust to the ground, and he recited:

In Winter, Coyote's belly is full of green fruit. When he tells a new story something ripens.

He is hungry.

"I told about Winter," he says. "I told about Spring."

His stomach groans. "I did not tell about Wind and River, the Inventors." He waits. "Good."

Marvin asked, "You want to hear this, Luke?"

"I'm listening," Luke said.

"No more room on my lap. Sorry."

"It is this way," says Coyote: "Wind and River are always jealous of each other. Wind sings. River sings. River carves. Wind carves. Wind invents flight. River invents float. This goes on and on. They make peace, invent Canyon.

"Canyon rends wind, bends water. They fight again, make peace, invent Ice.

"Ice angers Bird and Fish. They fight again. It goes on and on.

"I, too, get cold. 'It is time,' I tell them, 'to make peace.'

"Foolish Coyote, *Wind says,* I am full of needles because of your brother Cholla.

"Because of your cousin Peccary, *says River,* I am full of leeches.

" *'And you complain?' I say. 'Because of both of them, I am full of lies.'*

"*I howl over the water. I cry into the wind. They feel sorry for me.*"

Marvin said, "Clair, be a good listener. Are you listening?"

"Yep."

"Luke?" Marvin asked.

"Every word." Luke glanced at Ruth, her eyes closed in concentration. Clair's were the same, but Luke thought he saw Marvin's eyelids neither closed nor opened.

"*Wind checks his store of seeds. River sucks upon some of them. She spits some on his banks. She swallows others. Finally, she says,* This one.

"*It is the persimmon.*

"*Four seasons later, a persimmon seedling. Four seasons more, a tree. Years, there is peace between the Inventors.*

"*A mild Winter comes. A friendly Spring.*

"*River complains,* The roots undermine my banks. They muddy me and slow my carving.

"*Wind growls,* The limbs and leaves muffle my singing.

" *'That is all?' I say. 'That is all?'*

"*They argue. They fight. I want to laugh but I should not laugh, so I fill my mouth. When it is time, I will make peace again between them.*"

Coyote smiles. "A good story?"

He answers himself. "A good story." He belches.

His breath smells like ripe persimmons.

After the story, Clair wanted to ride some more. Marvin lay on his side. She pointed at his stomach.

"I just *told* you a story," he said. He made a persimmon-gulping noise, and then all four of them made the noise, competing with each other for the funniest version.

Ruth took Clair into the hut and came out with a shawl and blanket. She bunched up the shawl and put it under Marvin's head, then she covered him with the blanket.

"Is he okay?" she asked Luke.

Uncertain whether she meant Marvin or Michael, Luke answered, "I don't know." Clair climbed into his arms and they played Try This One On.

Later, the child sat in the dust near Marvin's head. She had taken a mesquite twig from her pile of treasured dolls and toys and now she tapped it against the ground. Almost inaudibly, she sang fragments of the Tewa song Ruth had taught her.

"What'll you do?" Luke asked, sitting next to Ruth.

She lifted her head and closed her lips against a bitter grin. "I've already decided. Buy my cameras back from Mary's Pawn." She turned her wrists in her lap as if to look at the small blue veins meeting the deep wrinkles of her palms. "The *Sun-Bulletin* will take me back."

"It's a good little paper," Luke said. They both smiled at the lie in that, and that helped Luke relax.

Clair tapped the twig against the dirt near Marvin's head. Fascinated by her own singing, she rocked her small head.

"You know about notching, Ruth?" Luke shifted his long legs in the dirt, bit his heels in. "An old 'bo told me. In the Thirties the hobos and folks who were 'on the bum' and hopping on and off trains knew which houses they were welcome in. A 'bo always made a little notch on the fence or gate or someplace if he was fed there. Other 'bos would see the notch and know those folks kept aside some of their food just for them. One house might have a lot of notches. One house, none.

"This valley," he said, "was notched from one end to the other. It was the kindest valley anywhere."

Luke raised his knees to push his shoes deeper into the dust. "Maybe that's part of how I turned into a 'bo. I lost my bakery job one morning without even getting a week's notice. I got mad and walked the length of the rails through the valley. Nearly every old house and dirty, broken-up shack— notched. And all these pecans to filch, with all the orchard owners ready to look the other way."

"Different now?"

"Well, not just the valley. This is a different world. Fearful. Untrusting."

Clair had stopped singing, but she tapped her stick softly against the ground, her arm tiring.

"Clair," said Ruth.

"He's sleep," the child said, nodding at Marvin.

"You can stop."

"Okay." Clair came to Luke. She sat on his knees, and he raised her up and lowered her. "Go bumpteelou," she said. He did it again.

Ruth said, "Mr. Sovel told you that? About notching."

"Bumpteelou," said Luke, pretending not to hear.

11

I needed to memorize it, Mom said. About the war in heaven and Michael beating the dragon and the words of testimony from bloody lambs or sheep or some bloody something or other that was bloody. I can't remember.

The lantern had been growing dimmer and dimmer for two hours. Finally, the light went out. Assembling the next level of scaffolding, we didn't speak. The darkness of the smokestack at last equalled the soundlessness. The soot baked into our safety glasses blinded us more, but it would have been dangerous to take them off. We groped for the scaffolding. Afraid of burning ourselves against the close walls, we fit the pipe ends by sense of touch, by joining our fists just a certain way. When we safety-chained the corners, the clinking echoed and returned, sounding like the groaning of ship chains.

We fit the standing boards in and sat on our pneumatic hoses. We groped for the lunchboxes that we had so lovingly carried up the six levels of scaffolding; they were both just identical metal boxes, but we petted them like fat smooth lizards until we each had chosen the right one. With my mask off, I couldn't catch my breath in the volatile air, so after every bite of food, I held my mask on in order to chew and swallow. It was slow, nauseating effort.

We weren't sitting more than two feet apart, but I never heard Matthew's mask-screened hissing change. "You there?" I asked.

"Who?" he said.

"Are you eating?"

"Now?"

"Are you eating, Matthew?"

He snapped his lunchbox closed. "Done."

"Like hell." When he didn't answer, I said, "If you can't eat, drink some water at least."

"Michael, if you can't shut—wrong—up—then—hell—shut up!"

"Drink some water, Matthew. You're not even making sense."

He drew a deep breath and released it in a trembling wave. "Finished?" he asked.

"No," I said. I strapped on my mask. My own breath formed a smothering hand over my mouth.

"Finished?"

"No, dammit, I'm not, and you better—"

"Finished."

"Matthew?" I reached into the dark where I thought he sat. When I had found his pants legs and then shirt, I realized he was curled on his side. Reaching for his head, I placed my hands on his helmet.

"Mask—a wrong—a broken—"

I turned him on his back and took his mask off. I put mine over his face. "Matthew?" I fit his mask over my face.

It worked okay. "Drink some water. Please God, drink some."

I forced the top off the large metal water container and dipped a thermos cup in. He pulled the mask down and guided my hand and the cup to his mouth. "Let it stop," he said. "Too much." He sucked at the cup and, when I gave him more, he guzzled.

"Something's wrong with you, Matthew," I said. Taking off my gloves, I poured water over his neck and undid his asbestos jacket to pour some over his chest. I lifted my safety glasses to try seeing him, but it was no good. "Matthew," I said, "something's wrong."

When I lifted him into a sitting position, his left arm fell and, though he could draw his right leg up, his other lay straight. I drew his face up to my chest and tried to touch him under the glasses, the mask, the helmet strap and jacket collar.

I couldn't touch him whole—that's what I remember: that I couldn't place my hands over his whole face and feel that he would hold together.

"Finished," he mumbled. "Finished. Finish." The brick dust had hardened the hair near his forehead and ears; it had hardened his stupid, stringy moustache; the starch at the corners of his mouth was stiffening. Becoming a kind of stone or statue, Matthew pressed his head into my chest. His mumbling stopped. His head and shoulders stiffened in that position. With my fingers at his lips, I could sense his breathing.

"No!" I called out. I put him down again on his side. Into the echo of the word "No" that blasted the complete darkness above and below us, I shouted, "God! God! God!"

I knew it would take an hour or more to build scaffolding to the top. I screamed and wept and begged God to *lift* us out if you're God, take us out *now* if you're God, please!

Almost falling, I bumped the water container. It plunged through the hole at the scaffold's center. The rope attached to it whipped over the rough board edge in a horrible sound like a curtain ripping. When the rope end caught, the dead weight of the container made only a slumping noise.

I shouted down the throat of the scaffolding for the God of whatever he was the goddamn god of to hear us, to help please help. I cried. I folded myself around Matthew and I remember I started shouting, "What? What?" Maybe I was shouting at Matthew to say something or God to please speak. It could've been I was shouting at them both. Then, placing Matthew more safely on the board, I threw the jackhammers through the hole of the scaffolding, cut the hoses and the ropes attached to everything, and was not surprised by how the crash of the equipment was muffled by the brick six stories beneath us.

I understood again how impossible it would be for us to go back down and dig through all that brick in order to get out. Kneeling to reach him, I said, "Matthew, I'm taking us out." Unable to know if he heard me, I started building the next level of scaffolding.

·

On New Year's Eve morning Luke woke to the sound of Clair singing and giggling, standing over him. "Good morning, you silly bird," he said and tried to nudge his head out of her hands.

"Birds sing," she said, as if telling him the deepest secret.

"Sure do," said Marvin.

Ruth woke up. "Clair?" she said.

"Birds sing," Luke said.

"Birds sing," said Clair.

Ruth's half-smile raised her chin only a little and brought no color to her face. Luke thought she looked as if she had been crying.

Marvin raised his head into the air and yipped. He snapped his teeth near Clair and said, "Fresh birdsong for breakfast!" He snapped again, crunched and chewed loudly. "More!" he said, and Clair went to him and sang more.

"Ruth," said Luke, "I could take Michael some of the stuff we have from the store. Maybe we could both go."

She leaned her back against the hut wall. "Luke," she said, "do you understand all of this?" She folded her legs under her and brushed dust from the jeans she wore. "I'm a thirty-year-old woman—locked out of my own house."

Luke asked Marvin to take Clair outside. Wrapping the child in a blanket, Marvin put her on top of his back and crawled from the hut.

"If we went to see him . . ." Luke said, "we could. . . ." It didn't convince even him. "He just needs time, Ruth."

"I know." She rose, walked from the hut.

Following her, he said, "In a few days, Michael says."

"Tomorrow will be another year." She held the ends of her rebozo in her fists. The irises of her deep brown eyes were like empty nests.

"Look, Ruth, even he doesn't know this, but look what he's doing. In my family no one plays to win. Not off the basketball court, they don't. No one. Michael wants to win."

She leaned far into herself. She sat down against the north wall of the hut. "I love him."

"He wants to win." In saying it, Luke realized something more. Ruth was ignoring him now, folding her arms over her raised knees, furling herself into a tightening knot.

"I have to talk to him, Ruth."

The sun had brightened and sharpened the peaks of Sierra de la Soledad. Luke knocked again. "Michael? It's me."

From inside, maybe the kitchen, came his brother's voice. "Ruth?" At the door, Michael said, "Luke. It's you."

"Ruth's still at my place. And Clair."

Michael asked him in. "You can't stay." His face had grown more sallow since the last time. His lips were bitten, the lines around his mouth deep and straight. "Well. Hi. Coffee?"

"Anything. Sure, coffee."

"Good." Michael held the coffee pot under the faucet; he seemed to strain to hold the pot as it was filling. "Well?" When the pot was full he put it on the stove and said again, "Well."

"You're not looking too good, Michael."

"Thanks."

"You're welcome."

They sat at the table where Michael had been working. "How are they?" Michael asked.

"Clair is fine. She's found a best friend in Marvin. Marvin, too." Luke wondered if he should say anything about Ruth, but he knew Michael would ask anyway. "Ruth says to tell you she loves you. She said when this is over—she said for me to tell you this—she wants you to stop thinking you have to be strong for both of you."

Looking over the sheets of paper on the table before him, Michael said, "I'm almost ready."

"You look like you're not eating."

"I'm not boozing. If I look bad it's probably because I'm not drinking."

He wished Michael would look up from the table. "What are you going to do with all this when you finish?"

"Don't know. Any ideas?"

"How much longer? Do you know?"

"No."

"Michael. I've got to tell you something." He knocked on the table. "You listening? Listen, I love your family. It's felt good to have them for my own." That wasn't what he had meant to say. "I'm different, I think. I can't figure out how such a little time can do that. Everything's made me think about us—you and me—too." He couldn't be sure Michael was listening.

"Michael, none of us wanted to win, I don't think. We kept all our winning on the basketball court. And Matthew—"

"You won. Left. Lived on your own terms."

"That's what I told you and Matthew."

Michael looked up from the table. He took Luke's forearms into his hands. "It's going to work out, Luke. You believe me."

"Michael, you *want* to win. The hobo life, the trick, that was all a stupid, pointless win. Little wins. That's what I got all my life. But now you, your family. . . . Marvin and Eva. Romelia." Luke raised his arms up a little. He wanted to show Michael how they held each other's arms.

"Romelia?" Michael said.

"A long story."

Moving his head in a kind of back and forth trembling, Michael said, " 'I'd be lying if I didn't tell you the moon flips heads-or-tails every dust storm.' "

"Huh?"

"That's out of one of the letters you wrote me and Matthew. You remember the letters, Luke?" Michael looked through him to another Luke. "Matthew and I used to read your letters until they were rags," he said. From memory, he recited: " 'I'd be lying if I didn't tell you the leaves on every tree in the valley change color on the same half hour of All Souls' Day. They fall off at sunset, rumble every building off its foundation.' "

"You saved them?"

"I've been reading them through again. They're damn fine, Luke." The shadows under Michael's eyes and around his mouth deepened with a heated redness.

"You never wrote back. Just Matthew."

"Wanted to." Michael's hands weakened around Luke's arms. "Couldn't."

"Listen, Michael. I thought if I could get you here—both of you—" Luke felt his arms being given back to him.

"He loved you, Luke. He had a capacity for that, you know, bigger than any McWelt."

"*Save* us all, that's what I thought I could do."

"Just stay a little bit, okay, Luke?"

Michael poured the coffee into cups. He brought out a packet of letters from behind some pots in the cupboard. "Read that top one," he said.

10-7-77

Guys,

Got your letter, Matthew. Do I ever get one from what's-his-name? Is Mom okay?

It's chile season here in Enchantmentland. Trees are changing color, air's freezing Old Lady Romelia's underwear on her lines. She hides them on the inside lines, but I'd be lying if I didn't admit I watch for them. You can believe me. An old lady with lacy stuff, peach-colored and pink and some the color of gold leaf.

Cactuses shrinking all over the desert. Prickly pear and cholla and ocotillo smaller than they were two weeks ago. Tiny. Have I told you before? They start to wrinkle a little, get real thin, pretty soon all the arms and stuff are invisible. You have to see it or you ain't going to believe me, are you?

What's taking you so long?

December, everything all over the desert is miragey, see-through all morning, more real in the day. By five you could pass your fingers through even the mountains which, honest to God, are half the size of the clouds. I would've wanted to show this to Dad.

And me, I'm shrinking—right under four feet tall about now. Would I lie to you?

How much money you guys have to save before you come? Do I have to come to Ill. to get you? I'm not going to.

Make it a goal—after Christmas, okay?

Okay?

Luke

As always on New Year's Day, only a small crowd gathered at Bogel's to see the trick, which was particularly a shame because Luke had rarely sent the ball so high or rattled it that perfectly dead on the end of the yardstick. Enjoying his own precision, he took more risks. He boomed the ball off the pavement so hard he felt the veins thicken in his arms.

"Before it comes down," he said to the crowd, "tell me—"

Eva appeared on her bicycle. When she dismounted, she patted the handlebars as if she were stroking the nose of an uneasy horse. The basketball came down. Boom! he sent it up again. "Tell me—about the buds," he asked the crowd. "Before it comes down, tell me why there are buds on the ball." The ball shivered and spun and fabummed off the pavement once and he boomed it into the air, then out of sight, in the sun. "Because—"

"Easier to handle," said Eva.

"That. Okay, that." Without looking at her, he said, "But!" and built a pavement-banging dribble into another space shot. He spoke quickly: "Everything–that–vibrates–jumps–in–its–skin—The–court–bumps–up–and–ripples–where–you–dribble—." He sent the basketball up again. "The–backboard–goosebumps–every–shot–and–the–metal–of–the–rim–and–the–seats–where–you–sit–and–the–Coke–that–you–sip–in–the–stands—And–only–the–basketball–had–them–all–along–had–the–bumps–in–your–hand–in–the–air–in–the–coach's–locker–the–little–jump–in–the–skin–bumps–that–make–it—" The Voit slammed onto the yardstick. *Fututuhtuhtuhtuh*. It rocked there. "—make it more than what you think."

Futuhbumatuhbumatuhbumatuhbumatuhbum. Luke held his body, arms, and hands still. The ball stopped rocking. But it—Luke himself was sometimes amazed—it contracted and expanded on the poised yardstick.

"Like a great dam," Luke said. "Or a spaceship." He let the basketball breathe. He tipped the stick vertically, balanced the ball at the end. "The Voit," he said. "The Voit."

They filled his cup with bills. Eyes down, they said, "Great trick," "Your best ever," "Hard to believe." Henry Cabrera, the chiropractor, said in Spanish, "Sometimes I think I will cry seeing it."

Eva, standing behind the man, muttered, "¿Tres dólares por hacerte llorar? ¡Qué tacaño!" Three dollars for your tears? A cheat! The chiropractor shrugged and quickly walked away. Eva handed Luke a grocery bag.

Opening it, he found soft drinks, chips, bags of beer nuts, some large bottles of beer, and two or three cans of appetizer sausages. "I'll be," he said.

"The beer is especially for Marv—for el búfalo."

"Don't take off just like that, Eva." He put the bag down.

She lifted her right leg over the bicycle crossbar and rested her foot on the pedal.

"If I could see you, Eva, I could explain."

"Yes?"

"Can't I walk you somewhere?"

"You are courting me?"

"Yes. This makes it official, okay? Yes, I am."

"I like this." She smiled at her fingers closing over the handlebars. "Official." She rang a little bell on the handlebar. "Happy New Year." She waved her hand in the air and, at the intersection across the street, she turned her head to look at him and waved again.

"Come to dinner?" he shouted.

Her concentration slowly shifted to the stoplight. He called out again, "Come for dinner? Without your mother?"

"Yes," she answered.

Her head lowered slightly, she pushed off from the curb, and glided away.

12

I fought for a long time to construct the seventh level of scaffolding. At first, I was hurrying so much I clanged the fittings against each other and stupidly missed and hollered at the pieces when they fell apart. I took my padded gloves off so I could feel for the pipe ends, but I could only take the heat on my bare palms long enough to *almost* slip the pipes one into the other. Or, I'd have the ends loosely fitted and I couldn't grip the metal hard enough to push the pipe arm into the sleeve. When I reached down again for my gloves, they were gone from the boards.

Though the brick lining was cooler at this level than at other levels, the circumference was smaller and the heat rising from below us picked up force and speed as it corkscrewed upward on the way out of the stack. It made a churning I could hear even under my hood and hard hat. It drilled its way through me, hollowed me out until my arms and legs felt like heated metal pipe.

Afraid, I kept calling for Matthew to stay awake, to wake up, to—"it won't be long"—to "please God sit up god-dammit, Matthew, and quit scaring the shit out of me. I'm almost—I've almost—Come on. Please."

When I had the first wall of the scaffolding up, I shouted,

"See! Look, we can go up on two walls. We'll go up and out of here two walls and a floor at a time. Screw the other two, huh, Matthew?"

I said or I think I said—I talked basketball to myself: I'm going to drive left—backhand the pass. You hit me under and behind and I'll—here.

Raising the second scaffold wall, I felt my hands tearing on the spurs on the metal pipes but I was able to hold the ends and sleeve them. "In!" The word reverberated in me and choked off my breath.

I put up the standing board at the next level. I carried Matthew over my right shoulder and up. As my breathing returned to normal, I began to imitate the basketball crowds for him. Through the mask, in the echoing smokestack, the sound came back to my ears like the cries of a thousand people: "McWelt! McWelt! McWelt!"

The churning of the heated air and my own cheering and pained breathing formed the crowded gymnasium around me. I saw the time clock with the seconds left in the quarter. I saw the referee bobbing his head at his watch. I saw and heard the crowd on its feet. They screamed at him, "McWelt! McWelt! McWelt!"

My fingers gripping the pipes of the scaffold, I imagined myself sending a pass into Matthew's hands above his head. I watched the pass reach his fingertips, his hands whip back and forward once like the head of a striking snake, the ball backspinning as it sped in a line drive at the rim and then through and, jerking the net back, being swallowed in that sound the strings make. You could hear it through the clapping and seat-banging and shouting of "McWelt! McWelt! McWelt!"

I could hear it in the smokestack, hear that sound the strings make: the final breath. The very last.

.

In the evening as Luke walked back with the bag of food Eva had given him, El Cerro and the whole Black Mesa brooded under shifting fog. Through the dark limbs of the pecan trees, he called, "Ruth—Marvin. I'm back."

Inside, a hastily written note on a piece of cardboard lay on the floor.

Marvin bad. At hospital.
Ruth

Romelia answered her door as she always did, drawing Luke inside by his arm before saying hello. She explained that she had telephoned in the afternoon for the cab which took Ruth, Clair, and Marvin to the hospital. "You and Eva," she said, "vamanos."

Together on her bicycle, Eva and Luke rode on Highway 28. She sat on the handlebars, turning often to look at him. On the bridge over the Rio Grande separating the Stahmann orchards and Fred Huff's farm, he stopped.

"Tired?" she asked.

"No."

She climbed off the bike. She put her hand on his shirt near his heart.

"Okay, I'm a little tired. Scared about Marvin. I'm like a thirteen-year-old, huh?"

"Your ears are red."

"Well, I really stopped because of a question I've got."

As if sensing his helplessness, she smiled. "Okay."

"Okay." Holding her shoulders, he stood apart from her in the darkness and he looked closely. "You only ever wear two outfits. Down to your shoes."

"It is all I have."

"You come right out of the air."

"Hoop. If you know everything about me, all of it, what will you know?"

"More than nothing, for God's sake."

"More nothing. And what do I know about you, Luke?"

He put his hands around her waist and lifted her onto the bicycle handlebars. "You're here in Las Almas because of your mother?"

He began pedaling again. "Am I right?"

She nodded.

Past the protection of the pecan orchards now, the bicycle wobbled in the strong, cold wind that was chewing the fallow chile and cotton fields. She did not turn around to face him again until they came to the intersection of University Avenue and Highway 28.

"I missed her," Eva said. The slight bones around her temples and eyes seemed to emerge, and he was certain she would tell him everything now. "And I wanted to make some things right. Some things were not right." She turned away and concentrated on the road before them. "Do you understand?"

They bicycled over the railroad tracks. Farther up University Avenue, near the hospital, he stopped the bicycle again. Luke said, "He's in a warm room, anyway, right?"

13

The dust around me glinted. I thought it had to be almost sunrise.

Ten feet from the lip of the smokestack, I lowered Matthew from my shoulder to the small board beneath us. I looked down the black tunnel of our scaffolding. When I think about that now, I remember it was magnificent. I would have dared God right then and there to disprove that a man could build with his hands the grinding cylinder of a tornado or the gyre of cells that forms the ring in a tree.

I put my hands on Matthew's silent chest. For a long while I stared past my hands and past his body at the awful miracle of our work.

When I looked up, I saw a cone of golden-red light on the bars of the short iron ladder above us. It looked warm.

"Morning," I said to Matthew.

I worked slowly. Taking first his jacket and then shoes and pants off him, I balled them up and bound them inside his helmet. I took the glasses and the gas mask from his face, but everything was still too dark to see him. With one left-handed hook shot, I sent the helmet out of the smokestack. Then I lobbed my own glasses, mask, and helmet out.

Lifting him onto my left shoulder, I found a rung above me, locked my hands around it, and then slowly brought my left foot to the same rung. I don't know how I finally managed the impossibility of getting completely onto the ladder, but when I did straighten up I could not look down again. After two more steps I stretched my head into that cone of goldenness. At the very top, I lifted my leg over the smokestack lip and onto the first rung of the external ladder.

In the wavering vapor just above the mouth of the smokestack, crystalline particles of ash were melting heavy snowflakes as they collided. The rungs beneath my safety shoes were icy. I remember becoming angry halfway down at how snow was collecting on Matthew's back and neck. I shrugged him into better position on my shoulder, drew his head against my heart, and held it there the rest of the way to the bottom.

.

The elevator stopped at several floors before reaching the ninth. The young nurse at the reception desk said Marvin was in a room at the end of the hall to the left. "No need to knock," she said, "he's alone. And could you keep the door closed? He makes noises." She sat down to press the Hold button on a purring phone. The paper on the clipboard she handed Luke said "Register."

Luke printed "Hoop McWelt" on the ruled line and started to make up a telephone number for the space next to it. "Eva, can I put down Romelia's number?"

She wrote the number down for him and handed the clipboard back. The nurse thanked them.

"How is he?" he asked.

"Hello," the nurse said into the phone. Listening to the caller, flipping cards in a file before her, she glanced at the register. "One moment, Mr. McWelt," she said and, into the phone, "He'll be in for his rounds at six. Usually six. Thank you." She put the receiver in the cradle and looked at it.

"So, how is he?"

She said he would have to speak with Marvin's doctor.

Luke leaned over the counter. "Lady, come on. You know me. I know *you*. I've seen you watching my basketball trick at the mall." She looked up at him but not into his eyes. "I'm not asking for more than loose change, lady. Unless you tell me you can do my friend some good, I'm taking him home right now."

"He's very ill."

"Well?"

She looked at Luke's name again. "The doctor says no chance."

"Thanks." When they got to the room, Luke started to knock but changed his mind. Eva asked to wait outside.

"Marvin," Luke said as he walked in, "you aren't any prettier, I guess, but you don't look much worse." In fact, Marvin's face was horrible; his forehead and cheeks were hard and damp and swollen beyond the plane of his nose.

"Happened quick," Luke said, still pretending calmness. "You were doing pretty good the other day." The chrome bed rails, headboard and white bed linens shone under the fluorescent ceiling lights and bright table lamp. "Want me to shut some of these lights off?" He hit three of the four wall switches. He sat Marvin up and pulled the sheets more comfortably around him. "You're already dressed?"

Marvin's hard, gray lips formed a straight-line grin.

"Eva's with me. She's coming." He picked up the dish-washer boots. "You want these on? Could I help you with them?" He uncovered Marvin's feet. They were smaller than he had thought. "You've got us worried a little." He laced the boots and pulled the sheet over them, but that didn't look right. "I'm going to take you home." Putting his arms around Marvin's shoulders, he said, "I'll never be able to help you. Can you walk?"

Marvin lowered one foot to the floor and staggered into Luke, almost knocking them both down.

"I can get us help. Here, Marvin, I'll lay you back down." He asked if Ruth and Clair were somewhere in the hospital.

"Down."

"Downstairs?"

Marvin nodded.

When Eva came in she was pushing a wheelchair. She helped Luke ease Marvin into the seat. She asked where Marvin's socks were, did he put boots on him with no socks? "Marvin," she said, "I'm here, querido," easing the boots off him to dress his feet the proper way.

Pushing the wheelchair past the busy young nurse and into the elevator and then to the hospital lobby, Luke left them to look for Ruth and Clair in the hospital cafeteria.

They were sitting alone in one corner of the room, Clair asleep in her mother's lap. Their clothing was dusty and wrin-kled, their faces and hair unwashed. Like bums, he thought. They'll scare off cafeteria customers. And the thought gave him some strange comfort.

Carrying Clair through the corridor, he looked at Ruth. "You tired?"

She whispered, "Frightened."

He gathered Clair's arms from her sides to her chest and held her closer to him. "We're taking Marvin away."

"To our home," said Ruth. "I called Michael. He said we should bring Marvin to the trailer."

At the cab, Eva and the driver had already laid Marvin in the back seat. She took Clair from Luke's arms and got in the front with Ruth. Kneeling on the floor of the cab, Luke began to smooth out Marvin's clothes. He couldn't think what else to do. He said, "Marvin, I'm making you look better is all. I'm—see?—I'm going to straighten you up some." He tucked in his shirt, pulled Marvin's sleeves over his arms and smoothed the cloth.

"Soful," said Marvin.

Without considering, Luke said, "Yeah? Yeah, Marv, it's me."

"Soful."

"Yeah? I'm making you look sharp." He moistened his palm and pushed back the hair from Marvin's temple, which had pulsed angrily before but now seemed bloodless, as if it were shrinking against his skull. "All I'm doing is I just want you to look nice, Marv."

With his fingers, Luke tried to spit-clean Marvin's face, but he rubbed at his hands with little success. "There. Sharp," he said.

At the trailer, the cabbie wouldn't take their money. "I give my prayers," he said in Spanish. He turned off the ignition and got out to help.

Michael wrapped a worn quilt over Marvin, carefully arranging it around his throat and chest. Before he and Luke could lift him into their arms, Marvin exhaled a kind of laughing whoop. Then his shoulders shook as if he were laughing again, deep inside himself. He stopped breathing. "Wait," said Luke. His shoulder pressed into Michael's chest. He could feel the solidness of his brother against him, cushioning his own trembling.

Together they knelt over Marvin. Michael said, "Go ahead. Go on, Marvin." He reached over and closed Marvin's eyes.

Luke asked Eva and Ruth to take Clair inside.

The cabbie said, "I will drive him. You send me where I go."

Luke sent him to the Fortham Funeral Home, where, a long time ago, he and Sovel and Marvin had gotten free food at the open-to-the-public wakes. "You tell Mr. Fortham that Hoop sent this man. He knows who I am."

14

Two days later, on Friday morning, a professionally lettered sign was posted on the front lawn of the Fortham Funeral Home:

Wake
OPEN TO THE PUBLIC
Marvin Rill
Autumn Rooms
4 p.m.

In the funeral home's old '62 Cadillac, Ruth drove Michael, Luke, and Eva to the San Albino Catholic Cemetery, where Mr. Fortham's two middle-aged sons had dug the grave for no charge.

The men met them at the gate, where the younger-looking of the two explained, "We already lowered it in. Is that all right?"

Ruth nodded. "You're kind to help this way."

The older of the brothers pointed at Luke. "You're the Hoop."

"That's me." Luke introduced everyone. He said, "Look, guys, my brother and I want a favor. We want you to leave us the shovels so we can come back after the wake thing and fill the hole, just us."

That was agreeable to them, the older one said. "Mr. Hoop, I know—my Dad said—this must have been a good man."

After the Fortham brothers left, Eva and Ruth went to the grave, leaving Luke and Michael at the iron gate. Holding the bars of the grill, pushing his chest hard against them, Michael said, "I tell you what, I bet my shoe leather he was no Catholic."

.

I told Matthew about my hands. My palms were cut and bleeding. "They hurt," I said. I had been talking to him for all nine stories down the external ladder.

"Matthew," I said as we descended, "Matthew, we're back." I couldn't hear myself speak. "We'd better get out of this snow—and noise!"

I was cradling him in my arms now. I shouted, "Matthew, listen to me. I'm—damn, you're heavy!" I laughed. I shook snow from my head and then brushed it from his. Matthew's mouth hung open like someone hollering "No," but the skin of his closed eyes was like the collision of a petal with a clear pond.

"I'm taking you to the tool shed. The big one." Why did I talk and talk like that? Carrying him badly, I walked across the shipping yard of sheet-steel coils. The grit-baked lamps hanging on wires over the yard cast a dirty light through the heavily falling snow, and the slightest breeze jumped shadows away from and onto our path.

"There—right there." The main tool shed entrance was open; behind the supply table a barrel fire burned. "It's quiet again," I told Matthew.

I dragged tarps from the supply shelves and eased him down on one of them near the fire. I covered him with another. Pretty soon, the ice in his chin-beard melted away and the snow that had gathered in his hands dissolved. His dark brown hair, even the lighter hair at his brows, was wet. I wiped his face clean.

.

Around noon, Luke used Mr. Fortham's telephone to call the Gospel Rescue Mission. He asked Katherine Arrowen to get out the word about Marvin's wake banquet.

"Done," Katherine said and then, shyly, "Do we have to come to the funeral?"

"You already missed it, Katherine."

"Sorry."

Since the Mission was on Griggs, only four blocks away, the people living there came as a crowd. Luke knew most of them, though two of the families and a few of the couples might have been people he hadn't met before.

Katherine was there with Dibs, an alleyway entrepreneur who made money from selling paper, mostly newspapers he collected all over town or, according to his need, took from front yards and porches. Jerry was there with his white hardback Bible, a folded sack stuck between the pages. Luke knew *his* tricks: if he couldn't save some Mexican souls while they were waiting in line to be served, he would, at least, save some food in his doggie bag.

Agnes Sanchez, even thicker than usual, looked in good health. Yet, as she nodded hello to him, Luke sensed she was ashamed of being there. Like a coach signaling a bunt, she nervously touched her billcap and her shirt, then fingered the buttons on her sweater. Luke had known Agnes when she still owned the Winchell's Donuts on Boutz Street. Probably every hungry person in Las Almas knew her then. In 1978 when she lost the business, Luke had helped her; all the "walkers," all the 'bos had done what they could for her.

Luke said, "Agnes, come and meet some folks." At the table where Ruth and Michael stood ready to serve the food, Luke introduced her and announced that she would be the front of the line.

B. L. Bookwuller hurried behind Agnes. "How do," he said to Eva, who had just told Clair to be polite to everyone.

"How do!" said Clair, giggling at herself.

It caught on, and after that each person in line greeted Clair the same way. "How do!"

Dibs, at the end of the line, said it too. "She likes that," he said and then said it for himself, every bit as tickled.

Later, while others had seconds, Katherine slipped her arm into Luke's. Jealously, she asked, "That one," nodding at Eva, "is she with you?"

"Want to meet her?" Luke asked.

"Too late."

Luke could see he had guessed right. With second helpings in one hand and the white Bible open in the other, Jerry was reading something no doubt sacredly threatening to Eva and Romelia.

As Katherine and Luke went to their rescue, B. L. also walked over.

"They ain't saved," said Jerry to B. L. He turned to Luke and repeated, "They ain't saved."

Romelia calmly answered, "This is not true."

"Excuse my French," B. L. muttered, "but who gives a green crap?"

"God says, 'If—'"

"Jerry." Katherine bared her gritted teeth. "God says, 'Back off.'"

"Mmm-hmm," said B. L. "Let he who is without sin throw me his ham-and-swiss-on-rye."

At seven o'clock Michael asked Luke if he could see him a minute. They walked to the back of the funeral home and leaned against the garage door.

"Luke," Michael asked, "is this circus getting out of control?"

"You never know," Luke answered.

"What's Mr. Fortham going to say?"

"Michael, he's done these wakes for fifty years. He's seen some things."

As if to scratch his shoulders, Michael moved his back against the garage door. "Everything's okay then?" He pushed his hair down and back at his temples. "I should have gotten a cut."

"Me too."

"Luke," Michael said, pivoting himself closer, "we'll get a cut and new shirts. We'll ask Ruth—we can ask Eva if you want—and go see Mom sometime."

"Michael."

"Okay. But some time or other we'll see her, okay?" He knocked his shoulder against Luke's. "Scared you forgot how to say the rosary?"

"No."

"You got one?"

They both laughed. Michael said, "All these bums. Hobos. Whatever they are. Weird. I tell you, Luke, you should have seen—at Matthew's funeral—same thing. People I barely remembered: teammates, coaches, people like that. People I never saw in my life, some of them out of the stands. As if counting his points made them family." He stuck his hands in his rear pockets. "Steel mill guys like Stan and Howard came. Homo, too—Did you know him?—foremen like him came. And half the regulars from You Dam Right. They brought stupid horseshoe wreaths and they talked basketball and steel because—when people have nothing to say they sure say a lot of nothing, don't they? They didn't feel invited, they knew they weren't invited, most of them, but, you know what, they felt welcomed. Same kind of thing."

Listening to him, Luke had waited for his chance to say it: "I should have been there."

"Same thing, Luke, I swear to God."

"I should have been there for the funeral."

Michael stepped away from the garage door. "You're right. You should have." As they walked back inside, he said, "I'm going home with Ruth and Clair. I'll be back."

In a few minutes, he brought Clair to her uncle for a good-night kiss. "She sure loves you, Luke."

Luke kissed the top of Clair's head and said, "I love you too, Michael."

Clair whispered, "Love you."

"How do?" Luke whispered back, giving her back to her father.

The wake did eventually get out of control. Someone, a woman, thought it would be a good idea to sing. No one stopped her so she claimed the center of the room, cleared her throat, thrust back her shoulders, and began to sing a halting rendition of "If Love Is Good to Me."

Someone asked, "Who *is* she?"

Someone said she was a party crasher. Someone else asked, "When is she going to be quiet?" And an argument followed.

B. L. came to Luke to report that Jerry had followed a mission family outside and, though one of the children was sick—throwing up from eating too much—Jerry was "trying to redeem them like double coupons." B. L. then promised to round everyone up and head them back to the mission. He had little success, Luke noticed, until he enlisted the help of Eva and Romelia.

Dibs came up to Katherine and pestered her to dance with him. When she refused, he asked everyone still left at the wake, including Mr. Fortham. This is a wake, several people reminded him, a *wake*. "Be decent," Agnes Sanchez scolded him, but then she shrugged, threw up her hands, and went out with him to the courtyard.

Luke and Michael set about cleaning the room. Except to ask where chairs went or what should be done with the bags of garbage, they didn't speak. Finally, their work complete, they stopped to glance outside at Agnes and Dibs slow-dancing among the sculptured junipers. As Luke began to turn away, Michael whispered, "Hey. Don't." Reflected on the dark window, Michael's eyes met Luke's. "Just this once, okay, Luke?"

"All right."

The moment lasted past the nervous grins and flinches. Luke wondered if they had ever looked, just looked, at each other for so long. He was sure they had not. Never once on the polished boards of the basketball court or in the pews at church or at the dinner table in Meltenville. Never once in Las Almas at Michael's home or after Luke's trick or with Clair tumbling back and forth in each other's arms.

The longer Luke gazed at the two reflected faces, the less he could distinguish one from the other. He finally turned from the glass to squarely meet his brother's eyes.

"Michael," he said, "we can go and fill the grave now."

∎

This is one thing I remember, Matthew. This: I put your hands into the bowl of my gashed left hand, and the melted water from your palms soothed me. With my other hand I held my fingers over your eyes. I was afraid they might open again.

In every bottle—they have opened again. In every dream. In every station of my life. What is in them for a man who wants to suffer himself free of all this, Matthew? What do I see in your eyes? What do I see? I have learned.

Your best-ever looney look. Your forgiveness.